TABLE OF CONTENT

PROLOGUE

JODA

She inherited so much wealth after the father's dismiss, she fell for the wrong man, Denis who might be among the men that murdered her Dad because of his wealth and also ready to kill anyone that will be on the way of his victory.

She began to suspect Denise but afraid to confront him, she came in contact with a doctor who became her good friend but she hide her friendship with the doctor from Denis who was forcing marriage on her for his selfish purpose.

She became pregnant for the doctor while planning to marry Denis and none of the men knew about each other.

Not untill the whole secret leaked out and so was the bloody war that came with the whole drama.

JODA, Episode 1

My phone rang again as i step out of the bathroom, I quickly rushed to it, i smiled as i see the caller "Denis"

"Joda, where have you being...I have being calling you for long...

"ah ah, this was just the second time, I was actually in the bathroom, I even rushed out of bath knowing you are probably the one calling...sorry my love..

"what do you mean is just two times..i said i have called you severally... Do you want to start arguing with me over that or do i need to call you hundred times before you pick my call...I'm not one of your chykers, all those small small boys running around you...I'm your husband to be...hope you got that straight into your skull..

"I said i was sorry for missing your call, next time i will go to the bathroom with it...I'm sorry my one and only super hero..please don't be angry with me..

"whatever...anyway..I'm coming over to the house later in the day and i will be spending the weekend there, and i want you to buy chocolate Ice cream mix with vanilla, buy shawama and also Chapman drink, store it in the fridge for me, that's what i will be eating tonight, I don't want to eat anything else..

"okay..but i can actually make something good for us.. Since you will be here through out the weekend... Binta will also help out since she's around....we can eat home made food and go out tomorrow to Your favorite eatery...an..

"what home made food are you talking about Joda..? Your cooking is terrible and you know how much i hate your cooking..you are not a good cook..I told you that before...and I have also told you what i want tonight and also tomorrow we will still eat out...why are you trying to be stingy...you have the money...and don't ever argue with me over my demands....i don't like it...that's not right for a wife to be...

"alright..I'm sorry again...i will do as you ask..

"good..and before i forget tell the gateman to open the gate at my first horn i hate to horn twice...see you later...bye

The line went dead, and I just stood there looking at my phone in my hands, all i can think off is Denis constant demand and being so difficult to me, he was sweet and loving in the beginning, my father's P. A. Before he passed on,

everything was willed to me, being his only child, I gradually fell in love with Denis after dad's death, he was always there for me, comforting and supporting, he also told me how much he has always loved me for a very long time, and with time I fell for him because he was my companion, we dated for some time and Denis was so nice and he became the air that i breath and after which we started planning for our wedding, Denis changed gradually after our introduction and I got him his dream car on his birthday, he demand i put my house in his name, he said i should put the house that dad willed to me in his name because he cannot live in the same house with me knowing that i owe the place that he won't be comfortable living in it and being that i love him so much I called my lawyer and the paper was processed, I handed it to him and he was happy and our big wedding is coming up next month, he will be moving in next week, which i have looked forward to but Denis as much as i love him he sometime say and do things that hurts me, I'm ready to do anything for him but he throws my every mistake to my face nothing i do seems to make him happy this days, it worries me and i pray and hope he change if we get married, it will be difficult living with him if he continues this way.

I dressed up and drove out to get all we will need, my girlfriend stays with me and i also have house helps, who clean up the big house, I drove out with Binta my friend we stop at the fruit and vegetables shop, I have being shopping there for years and i have never met the owner of the place, but the workers there were so nice that always make me to tip them gladly, I have never met the owner of the shop, I always meet the workers, as i was picking things with Binta and one of the staff the owner appeared from inside, he introduced himself to us, he was a young handsome man, he greeted me warmly and told the staffs to attend to me very well, after getting all i wanted i waved them good bye

"Joda, that guy is so cute but he only fixed his eyes on you, he likes you do you notice that...

"shut up Binta , I'm almost a married woman, he saw my ring probably that's what he was looking at and i have being a good customer probably his staff told him about me that was why he was so cordial with us, and Denis warns me never to take off my engagement ring, and it has helped in putting guys far away,within a month i will be Mrs stop playing with my head and let Denis don't hear that from you or i have to explain myself, if you like the guy why not say and stop robbing it to my face ....i only love my Denis and no one can take his place in my heart...

"yes, I know but i don't really like that Denis, he can be so controlling I don't even know what you saw in him before falling in love, anyway My own is to be Chief bridesmaid, even if i talk from now to tomorrow you will never listen.. And yes i like that guy but he didn't really looked at me only got eyes for you ...

"thank God you know i won't listen so zip up your mouth...Denis is all i want, nothing will change that...

We drove down and got all Denis asked for before going back home.

JODA, Episode 2.

After getting everything we drove home, and i put everything in place expecting Denis, I was happy that evening, Binta was just looking at me and smiling

"you look so happy...hmmm, is it because your Denis is coming over...

"I'm always happy Binta, but yes I'm extra happy because of Denis..do you have any problem with that...and before you start lecturing me on my relationship...go and fix something for yourself in the kitchen...

"aah, Joda, what of all the things we bought, I'm already salivating waiting for mine...
"they are all for Denis, you never said you wanted shawama, all you asked for was Vanilla ice cream...all the shawama is for my love..
"lover girl... Anyway i thought you included my mouth in the...anyway i will even like to do some fruit salad for myself...but wait o Joda...I'm not lecturing...please... How do you even cope with Denis, on a serious note Denis is way too annoying whenever he is around, you are never yourself, all you do is try and please him which he never gets satisfied...i..
"Binta..stop it...leave me and Denis alone if you don't want to have issue with me...stay far off our business...we don't need your opinion in our lifes...stay off Binta.. I don't like it...
As i was still scolding Binta my phone started ringing, I rushed to my hand bag knowing it will be Denis and he won't be happy if i miss his call again, as i try to get the phone out, he cut the call i try calling him back..
"my love, are you on your way...sorry i try bringing out my phone from my hand bag before you cut off...
"Joda..why are you getting me pissed...how many times does it take you to get your phone from wherever it is...the phone rang severally again and you didn't pick up giving me another excuse just like in the morning...anyway I'm at the gate and i horn three times before the stupid security man opened the gate, I asked you to tell him to open up on my first horn but i horned three good times, Joda I need him sack immediately, if you don't do it

i will sack him myself...let him be replaced quickly to somebody who listens to instruction...

"is not his fault, the securities does their work well...i was the one that forgot to tell him...I'm sorry

He ended the call, and came inside

On seeing him i apologised again and he said he was tired of my constant "I'm sorry" I should stop pissing him off,

Binta stayed in her room, she didn't even come out after Denis arrived, probably she just wanted to stay in her lane like i warned her earlier,

After Denis freshened up i served him all he wanted, he was having a disgusting face as he unwrapped the shawama

"what is this...i never said i wanted shawama or is this for you...?

"but...but you called and said you wanted shawama, chocolate vanilla ice cream and Chapman...and i got everything..

What are you saying Joda..

He threw the tray of food to the ground, the whole ice cream that i bought and shawama spilled on the floor, he stood

"just simple instruction you can't follow...i said i wanted pizza and a chocolate bar not ice cream...i don't like ice cream, and worst of all vanilla flavor, where was your mind when i was passing the instructions...I'm freaking tired of this...i don't know if you just woke up today to deliberately spoil my day...now what I'm i suppose to eat.. And do not suggest making something....you know how much i hate your cooking...

"hmmmm...i...

"you want to say you are sorry again....please don't go there...is not too late...go or send someone to get me pizza that's the only thing i want right now and call those your maids to come and clean up this mess on the floor...i hate to see rubbish.....

"i wasn't going to say "sorry" I wanted to say that i heard you clearly on the phone mention shawama.... Denis, how do you always expect me to feel, most especially when you suddenly start hating my cooking, I remember my cooking use to be your favorite, what has gotten into you of recent, I do whatever you wanted, you wanted a brand new car and i make sure you have it, you wanted your name to be on this property, i decided to call my lawyer who processed the papers....what exactly is the problem...i do everything to show you how i much love you, yet you aren't satisfied....wha

"not everything Joda...your fathers company is still in your name, the other houses that are occupied by tenant is still in your name, many of his assets are all in your name...not mine.. The only one you managed to change my name to is this house, if you love me enough you will do more for me, prove it...

"I love you Denis does not mean that I'm stupid, come to think of it, all you care about is properties and my dad assets, do you love the properties or me, or is it the assets you only cared about...answer me Denis...because you are beginning to stress me out...

"ho..how can you say that Joda...you know how much i love you, is only work stress that is driving me nut this days... You should know me better...i appreciate everything you have done for me...I'm sorry for being over demanding....maybe you can bring the home made food if there's any available...i will eat it like that...but you should know I'm mostly stressed up this days... How can you even compare my love for you with your fathers assets he left for you....I'm not getting married to you because of that but for the love i have for you my darling wife...

"I Know is not stress from office work maybe some other work because you are the general manager of the company and I'm the managing director...we only go to the office twice in a week to foresee things, the staffs and managers there are doing great and reports to us if is beyond their control...but is fine I hate to argue with you...

"work stress with the upcoming wedding too , I can't wait to be officially husband to a beautiful lady, but when we get married you promise to make me the managing director, being a general manager is a small title to me. Remember I'm your husband...

We settled our differences that night, through out the time the argument was still hot Binta did not show face unlike her, she's probably angry with me, I love Denis, yes I really do but sometimes he can be so annoying but I'm willing to overlook only if he will stop making unnecessary demands

I always tell him my money is equally his but he should quit acting like a spoilt brat, I won't take that from him..i want a fairytale wedding and a happy life after with Denis....

JODA, Episode 3.

Denis has finally returned back to normal him that i use to know not the over demanding bully he wanted to turn himself into, he is so loving and less demanding now, we have a normal healthy conversation not the unnecessary argument,
Binta is still not lively like she use to be, when we are together,
I spent much time with Denis, don't really have time for anything or anyone, and even if me and Denis are sitting out or hanging out, and i ask Binta to sit with us or go with us, she sometimes decline if Denis is there, she is never comfortable around him,
Today Denis decided to ask me about her behaviour which is also pissing me off
"what is wrong with your friend, Binta... Do you notice that she never likes me, only pretending because of you...
"don't mind her... I really don't know what is wrong with her, I know she don't really like you...she even told me that herself, she also said you can be over demanding and annoying too, but I don't care what she says, you matters more to me than anybody...
"oh really...she said all that, she is very stupid for saying that, I'm happy you never listens to her, maybe you should change her from being your Chief bride maid to any of your friend, or even Vanessa, Vanessa is even more beautiful than she is, you can't have somebody that hates your husband around you, Binta is just jealous of you, she wish she has your kind of money or man, and

she will never be you, you are beautiful, smart, rich and intelligent, you also have me to compliment all your uniqueness...and i love you...

"I love you more, but I have already picked Vanessa as one of the bridal train, Binta has being my friend for long, and I can trust her because she has always being trustworthy, I don't know what got into her, I don't know why she doesn't relate well but i don't think is Jealousy, or probably you are right, she maybe jealous or something but Vanessa is not as close as Binta is... Since you want Vanessa...fine by me, I will just dismiss Binta..

That night as i slept, I had a dream, I saw myself walking down the aisle in my flowing wedding gown, I was all smile as i walked to where Denis stood, and the priest asked "is there anyone seated here that will not want this couple to be husband and wife, speak now or forever hold your peace"

As he said that, everywhere became silent, so silent that you can even hear if a pin drop, I scanned through the crowd, they were unknown faces, I didn't see Nobody that i know seated among them, and they were looking so sad, why are all this strange faces sad on my wedding day, where did they even come from" as i was still wondering about the strange sad faces, a man stood up from a distance, an elderly man, he was moving towards me but he wasn't walking, as he got closer and i saw his full face, I screamed in terror, "Dad" and woke up,

it was my father that stood up to stand against my wedding with Denis, My Dad has being dead for three years, he can't oppose my wedding with Denis who was his P. A, even the day he died in his office it was Denis that discovered his cold body lying in his office and raised alarm, my dad had a lungs cancer which after his visit to his medical doctor abroad, he was fine, he got better, and was back to work in his usual active mood, eating and doing what he love to do as before, he still take some vitamins and supplements just as he was prescribed to take, and was also warned to stay away from certain drugs, food and some other things, he followed every rule given to him not until that day, he never showed any sign of sickness in the morning or afternoon only to be discovered dead in the evening, during the close of work, right in his office,

autopsy showed that he was overdosed, how can dad overdose himself, I thought he was taking his drugs according to prescription, why did he has to take a killer drug to die, living only me, how would i have cope if not for Denis, mother died when i was still a little girl, father refused to remarry, he wanted to give me the best parenting, he said I'm like a million children to him, he also wanted to walk me down on my wedding day and hand me over to a good man who will cherish me like him, he wished to See Me happy and i have looked forward to making him proud until death snatched him away, I cried and couldn't eat for days, I wanted to die with him, life was so lonely without my loving dad, who toiled day and night just to give me the best,

He can't possibly say that i shouldn't marry his Personal assistant, who was among his close staffs, also among the people he trained and paid off their tuition fees when they were in school, my

Dad love Denis like his son and made him his P. A, after he graduated, Denis sometimes travels with him, my dad has changed Denis car twice, he was very kind to him and also other of his staffs, he will even be glad I'm getting married to him, Denis made me fall in love with him, he was so caring and loving after my dad's death, I was not dating him when dad was alive, but we started dating after his passing, Denis has being so cool, if not of recent he change to some strange being, but he is back to his normal self and I'm glad, I know it was a bad dream because dad will be happy I'm getting married to his P. A, who was like a son to him when he was alive,

I didn't tell anyone about the dream not even Denis, although i wanted to say it to him because i don't hide anything from him but something kept me from saying it,

Me and Binta drove out to get something and i decided to tell her to go because she's not happy with Denis and he isn't comfortable with her around, I told her Vanessa will take her place, I said in a way that shows how remorseful i was to let her go and surprisingly she wasn't angry,

"Hey....Joda...you have just saved me from a big stress...i have being thinking how i will be there...watching you marry that gold digger of a man...I'm sorry but this is not an insult and i know you will still tell him what i said because you are blindly in love, but i don't care...Joda...but your Denis doesn't love you but your money.... Don't think because he was your father's p. A and your Dad took him as a son and he was also the last person with your dad before he died and he has

being so caring since then....don't think because of that makes him the man for you, I dislike him and i just couldn't hide it... Please i ask of this one favour from you because you are my best friend and i wanted to be a sister you never had...please don't ever allow Denis to manipulate you in changing any other properties or your father's hard earned assets into his.. Don't let him do that even after you are both married because i see you are so sold out to him nobody can change your mind in settling with him , you are smart Joda, don't allow Denis to outsmart you if not your parent's death will all be in vain ,most especially your father who built an empire for you all his sweat will go down the drain if you allow Denis manipulate you, and he doesn't suppose to be in same house with you , why can't he wait after the wedding before moving in...anyway what is my own...I'm proud to say he isn't the man for you ...period, tell him i said that if you get back home...if he has liver he should come and ask me and i will be glad to tell him to go to hell, I'm sorry but i just have to say my mind, please before you finally dump me, let's go to that vegetables and fruit shop, I want to pick something that will at least be your farewell to me...
I was angry with Binta because of the things she was saying about Denis, they are not true , Denis is a nice person and doesn't love me because of any sentiments, but Binta is entitled to her opinion so i can't hate her, maybe Denis was right in letting her go, as much as i was angry I still manage to drive her down to the shop,

the fine young man who owns the place was around... I guess that was why Binta wanted us to come down here.

JODA, Episode 4.

"sorry, we didn't get your name the last time...
"Kuria...kuria Landy...that's my name... And yours..?
Before I could even open my mouth to answer Binta stepped in
"her name is Joda... Joda Tomas...that's her full name, mine is just Binta Greg, but wait you said your name is Korea Landing, ...what kind of name is that...is it like Korea Japan or Korea is landing...how can your name be Korea... Tell us little about yourself....are you a half cast...or fully from here...your accents is nice.... So Korea are you married or seeing someone....becau... Aaaawwwuuu.... Joda... Stop pinching me.....
I was trying to hush Binta to shut up and stop embarrassing the young man who was just laughing, when he laughed his gap teeth showed up with a matching dimples, I love gap teeth, and my Dad was blessed with one, one of his favorite features , I love making him laugh when he was alive so that i can see his fine gapy, I have wished severally to have one while growing up but my wishes never come true, Kuria's laughter was also making me to smile despite i was pinching Binta to stop teasing him
"no...is not Korea Landing...is Kuria Landy, I'm not yet married but will do that once i see who to

settle with, I was so much focusing on my business I didn't have much time for dates, now I'm fully established I will start working towards having a good life partner... Okay, let me tell you about myself, my Mom was a single mom and she wasn't from this part of the country, she gave me her family name, my Dad was from this country, was after she told me about him I decided to travel down in search of him but on getting here, when i finally found the family he came from, i was told he died eleven years ago, I decided to stay here, live here among his people who I'm also part off, my Mom later got married and had a new family, I visit them ones in a years, they are doing fine, but i have decided to live among my father's people, a father i never met but only through pictures that my Mom gave me, and i have being here for 9years, I started my business here, and business has being good, people over here love vegetables and fruits, wonderful people like you...
Before i could say anything again Binta spoke
"we are very sorry to hear about your dad, Joda also lost her father three years ago which still troubles her, so both of you are fatherless... Please don't take it personal is just a joke, but God has really blessed you in this land, looking at how stored up your shop is and how people patronise you, maybe is because of your fine look and... Aaaahwwwuuu! Joda that's painful...stop pulling my hair...what is wrong with you...I'm an adult, we are in a democratic world...freedom of speech...allow me to talk if you don't want to...don't pull my hair again or i will pull yours....
I have to drag Binta 's head hard for her to shut up,

"please, don't listen to her she can be a parrot sometimes, I'm so sorry for everything, I know that feeling of loosing a father, but is all good...I'm glad you are doing well for yourself here Kuria..

"I'm equally sorry for your lost...please you ladies should come around tomorrow, my place is just three buildings from here, I have a back kitchen and a sit out too, let me give you a treat of trequi....please don't say no...you will really love it,

"what in god's name is treku...whatever that is...it sound like a good win though, we will come...Joda don't really drink but she will love your trek...sorry I'm trying to call the name but my tongue is falling apart...

I don't know why Binta was too forward, especially in the presence Kuria, I don't really drink, how do she know i will love whatever kuria was offering us, I was just standing here and admiring his fine set of teeth with a gap in between, and his fine brown eyes, and a good accent makes me feel like I'm already cheating on Denis, in other to scare him off from me I used my ring hand which had my shining Diamond engagement ring to rob my face and stroke my hair, it looks funny but I didn't care I can't be tempted to cheat on Denis in any way, I did it severally and he noticed and smile before he spoke

"trequi..is not a win is a vegetable sauce mix with mushroom, one of my Mom best food, she taught me how to do it and i want to specially prepare it for both of you if you don't mind....and i have seeing your ring Joda...fine Diamond...an indication i should stay off...you are taken...i get the message very clear....Hahaha..is funny though the way you kept on doing that...I'm not gonna bother you or your friend...i just want to appreciate one of my constant customers, I knew you even before you do...sometimes i stay at that corner where no one sees me but i see everybody, I sit and watch how my staffs attends to people, sometimes I stay in my office and watch the CCTV camera, so i see regular faces and you are one of them...so please...you can even come with your husband or fiance...i will prepare enough for everyone to even take home...but no problem if you can't make it down...

"don't worry Kuria... We will be here...me and Joda are both coming for the trequi...we won't miss it..

We said our goodbyes and I drove home with Binta, I asked Binta why she kept on talking like a drunkard, embarrassing kuria and making me to start regreting of taking her down to his shop, she laughed and ignored my question, and only said I should get ready for tomorrow to be trequilize by Kuria 's food, I joined in and laugh because I will love to see him laugh and showcase his fine teeth with the gap in between, i will also tell him to teach me the recipe too if the food is nice so that i can prepare it for Denis but I'm still feeling guilty, my wedding is next month end and I'm admiring Kuria and getting all familiar with him, I quickly waved it off Kuria just wanted to appreciate his customers like he mentioned, he even said i can come with my husband to be, so that's cool by me, I will ask Denis if he will come with me and Binta to Kuria 's place.

Denis was not around when I got back, he didn't tell me he was going out, so i called him and a lady picked up, my heart skipped but was calm when i found out it was Vanessa, she said Denis car broke down, and she saw him along the road trying to call his mechanic so she gave him a lift, he was actually in the toilet when i called after exchanging pleasantries she handed the phone to Denis who was out of the toilet according to her, I was surprised to hear that his new car that isn't up-to a year suddenly broke down and Vanessa appeared like an angel and drove him to her place, but the sad thing is that he said he wasn't coming home that night , that ones his car is fixed he will be going over to his friends place, they planned to watch football together that night , i was angry and asked him why he didn't tell me all this before leaving the house or even to called me on phone, he apologised and said he tried calling me but my line wasn't going and his friends just called him immediately i left the house, he also reminds me of Vanessa being my Chief brides maid and i told him no problem, that one was already sorted,

after the call i called Binta to the room and told him to stay with me that Denis wasn't coming back that night, Binta was overjoyed and danced round the room, we gist that night and i also mentioned the dream i had about my dad to her, she said is an indication that my Dad does not support the wedding, she suggested we pray before sleeping which we both did,

I didn't believe Binta interpretation about the dream, she was only saying that because she does not like Denis but as i sleep that night all I dream is the trequi with Kuria and he was so full of smile, I actually thought that ones the day break I will tell

Binta that i wasn't going again but as I woke up in the morning all that was on my mind was kuria,
towards the afternoon we dressed up and i tried calling Denis but his line was off, probably after the long night of watching football with his friends he was tired and put off his phone to avoid being disturbed, so that he can sleep, I will try his line in the evening again if he didn't call,
When me and Binta finally got to Kuria's place he was wearing a kitchen apron, I laughed on seeing him look like that he also laughed,
there something about him that makes me feel happy, maybe because he shared the same shape of gap teeth with my late Dad, or there's more but I love the way i feel when I'm around him it also makes me feel bad, I feel like is unfair to Denis to be feeling this way with another man.

JODA, Episode 5

As we step into the house, Kuria's place was so beautiful, the architectural work was so fine, everything in the house was creative, I use to think my house is beautiful until i step into Kuria's place, even Binta was amazed at the beauty,
"your place is so fine Kuria, I'm serious...no joke this time, because even when I'm sounding serious Joda takes it for a joke, she can't even deferential when I'm joking and when I'm serious,but everything here is so creative, who did the interior decoration for you?

"thank you Binta...i did all the decoration, aside my vegetable business I'm also into interior decors and designs, so this place was done by me...
Me and Binta both explode with "wow" at same time. The guy is really good, you needed to see his place, I fell in love with the decorations and i asked him if he can do something like that in my place, I also told him I will pay any amount for it, he objected for sometime, I insisted with a plead, he later agrees to do that, I was happy, we exchanged numbers, I will call him ones i speak with Denis about it,
"joda, your house will soon change to new look with a touch from Kuria, but me...mmmh, ones me and James gets married I will talk to James about decorating our place too, I can't be left behind in the house deco thing, Kuria...you are really strange, your place is creative, haven't seen anything like this, your name is strange, haven't heard any name like that before and even your food is strange, trequi, have never heard of such, your second name should be called "strange man" anyway...i can't wait to taste your food before going to meet my James, who is already waiting for me, I just said I must not miss kuria's trequi...
I shaked my head for Binta who kept on talking, non stop, Kuria was only smiling as she babble, he took us to the back yard sit out which was also outstanding, he served us the trequi, which looks and smells great, it smells like mint, when i tasted it, it was okay too, Binta's phone was ringing non stop, she kept on ignoring the call as she enjoyed her food, I ate so slow with the fear it won't have a side effect on me, because my stomach easily

breaks loose, we talk as we all ate, Binta of course was the talkative in our means and Kuria was enjoying the whole attention she's poured on him, he sometimes looks at me in a way that makes me smile, he was fun to be with, after sometime Binta stood up

"I got to run Joda, James will be so angry if i don't see him again today, we actually planned to see today, he has being calling me, but relax and enjoy your trequi, Kuria obviously doesn't bite, he is a perfect gentleman, he will keep you company, I'm not sure of coming back today but i know you will be fine, I test James to come and pick me and he is almost here, thanks so much Kuria, please can i have one more plate of trequi for James...thank you. Joda feel free and be good...don't miss me"

Kuria gave Binta a pack which contains two plate of food, she thanked him again. Before sticking out her tongue to me, and stormed out, Kuria followed her, so that she won't get lost inside the house,

after seeing her off, he returned and sat opposite me, I also told him I was going, I couldn't stand his gaze any more, it was burning through my spine, he pleaded with me to stay a little while before leaving, is not like i really wanted to leave but Binta who was always talking on my behalf is gone, the environment was calm and i didn't know what to talk about again, I started wishing Binta has stayed, kuria later packs the plates to go and wash, I needed to do something so i asked him if i can be drying the dishes while he wash, he quickly agreed, so we did the dishes together, and i put it away accordingly, he was done washing and wanted to assist me in clearing up the table, as his hand touched my arm probably by mistake I felt like i melted inside, my heart double skipped and i heard this sensational feeling down my stomach, like a butterfly, we later got quiet, as we have being talking, him most especially, trying to keep me company, the cold kitchen became hot for me, I was so uncomfortable, I couldn't tell exactly how i feel, he noticed and asked if i was okay, I told him i wasn't feeling too good, maybe the trequi was taking effect on me, he laughed, I asked him where his toilet was he showed me and i quickly went in, it looks so comfortable in there, I wasn't doing anything but just sat there, my emotion were building so dangerously fast around kuria, and he was obviously careful so that he won't step on my toes, I sat there for sometime telling myself how stupid i was, "how can i even think of having feelings for another man when I'm getting married soon to Denis, the man i claim to love, I hated myself for feeling the way i was feeling, I was still in my sad thought when kuria called me from outside the toilet door asking if i was okay, I replied with affirmative, I told him i was good, I later came out, and told him i will be on my way, I thanked him for the food and entertainment, he asked me to come around sometime, and i promised i will, he walked me to the door, as i tried to open the door he held my hand with the door knob, he gently turned my face to him still holding my hand, I faced him, he was really cool to be with but only what i was looking at was his eyes and watch as his lips move, my mind was occupied with silent prayer, my emotions where still running wide, I could have

taken my hands from him but I was enjoying the moment,
"I enjoyed your company Joda, but you were cold after your friend left, I just want to asked again if you are alright"?
I managed to smile before saying i was fine, at that moment it was as if something got into me and I gently kissed his lips, and as if he has being wanting to do that but don't know how, as i tried to part lips he held onto me as if his life depends on it and kissed me so passionately,
Denis was totally forgotten at that moment, the only thing i can think of was the beautiful moment with kuria, i didn't want it to end, but i suddenly came to reality, as i got myself I quickly loosened from his grip,
"what just happened to me, this where the thought running through my mind as i stepped back from Kuria, who tried to apologize, as he tried to hold me again i slapped him, which i quickly regretted, he held his cheek in shock, he tried to apologize again despite the slap i stormed out and ran to my car, he was after me begging me to stop and kept on saying he was so sorry,
i started the car and zoomed off, I watched him from my car side mirror, he was standing at same spot holding his head in his two hands.
I got home as quickly as possible and Denis wasn't back, I Was feeling and smelling of guilt, it wasn't Kuria's fault but me, I just needed someone to pass the blame to, I really wanted the kiss, i have imagined it right in his kitchen, when only his smell and face filled my mind, I have wanted it before I ran into his toilet to see if the feeling will go away, I

slapped him because of guilt, I felt guilty for having feeling for another man, which Led to a kiss I have so much expected,
the truth was bitter in my mind but right there in my room I felt i have cheated on Denis for allowing a kiss with Kuria, how can i even face Denis, I may even confess my sins to him because i felt so bad, I tried to call him, I really need him home, I was sounding so uneasy as he picked and asked if everything was okay I told him "no everything wasn't fine i needed to tell him something, he said he was on his way home already before i called him.
I was pacing the house, I needed to confess to Denis of the kiss with kuria, it was unfair to him, he has never cheated on me and he will never do that why should i do that to him, kissing and allowing my feeling to store up for kuria was enough cheating and i plan telling it all to Denis, I will confess and beg him to forgive me
He drove in and Vanessa was with him, they didn't come down immediately from the car, I watched from my room window, and saw him kiss Vanessa inside the car before stepping down, my eyes grew big my mouth path way and i swallowed hard, I forgot everything i wanted to confess at that moment, maybe i was mistaken something, it wasn't a kiss maybe I'm going crazy, but Denis can't possibly kiss Vanessa who is suppose to be my Chief brides maid, my friend, Denis can't cheat on me i totally trusted him that was more reason i felt guilty for feeling the way i did for kuria, he can't cheat on me, no way, that is not even possible, not

with Vanessa or anybody maybe i didn't see right, something must have clouded my vision,
As they both came upstairs, laughing and talking at the same time, they suddenly stop on seeing me, Denis came to me and asked me what happened, I forgot about my confession and said i just needed him home that's all,
they both laughed and everything about confessing was forgotting but guilt was still eating at me, maybe i will tell Binta if she comes around tomorrow, Vanessa was all lively and friendly and wanted to be wherever Denis was, although I don't trust her but i trust my Denis.

JODA, Episode 6.

Me and Binta had a heated argument which almost led to a fight, after then we stopped speaking to each other,
It started the day she finally came over and I told her of the incident with Kuria, Kuria has being calling me that Even made me to block him on My phone.
" I cheated on Denis and the guilt is really killing me Binta, and i initiated the whole thing at first, I wish it can go away..it was unfair to Denis who was always faithful to me and never cheated, I felt so bad about that..
"Hold on...just hold on... You actually had sex with another Man, mmmh, I was even thinking you will never allow another Man close to you, any man that is not Denis is not Man enough... Cheating is

wrong but I'm happy you did it, I'm so happy you are breaking free from Denis grip, stop feeling guilty do you know how many women he might has slept with, he is not what you think he is.. Ooh so happy for the guy that got your heart, hope he isn't like Denis, who is this lucky Man, is he as fine as Kuria, ooh Kuria..that Guy is fine and creative, do you see his place that day, and his food was good James also love it, I forgot to tell you I stopped by to thank him he wasn't as cheerful as he use to be, he asked of you and I told him I haven't seen you yet, he wanted to say something else but stopped and flashed me a fake smile, I knew something was bothering him but he refused to say, I thought it got something to do with you..but it can't be, Kuria is the cutest Man alive plus My James minus your Denis, I'm joking o, your Denis is okay too but not like Kuria, maybe Kuria was having low sales that day... but there were lots of customers around as usual, maybe it was just a bad day for him, I even asked him and he said he was good, I should extend his greetings to you.. So i asked him when he will he making another trequi, he said that...

"Binta just shut up for ones, I'm telling you about an important issue and you are joking with it..be serious for ones please, you talk too much.. You are diverting from the issue at hand... I didn't lay with any man.. It was only a kiss.. We kissed... And the man was Kuria... After you left us.. You shouldn't have Left us alone that day..I felt stupid for doing that... I even slapped him out of guilt.. I regretted everything Binta, I felt really bad for having feeling for another man, which led to a kiss..it was really crazy...

" yes..you are obviously crazy Joda.. Oh My God, you kissed Kuria... Oh baby girl you have finally made me proud.. Although I wish it would have been More... But was it just the small kiss that's making you feel guilty... You are not serious... I actually thought you really cheated on Denis, My Joy would have being full, why do you have to slap that nice young man, you shouldn't have hit him because according to you, you initiated the thing, your feelings for him is mutual, he obviously has feeling for you too, now everything makes sense, it was because of you he was feeling sad that day...I see, but Kuria obviously loves you right from that first day we saw him, if you can remember I told you that day, I'm becoming a seer, call me prophetess Binta, because I saw this coming, so because you wanted me to babysit you that day, I should cut off My outing with my man, no way, your feelings are Strong For Kuria, nurture it and you won't regret it, listen to a prophetess like me.... if you want a fairy tale life go with Kuria but Denis will make you hate men... Break free from him now is not late... Joda seriously Denis is not the man for you, that man at the vegetable store is, Kuria is intelligent and hardworking, look at what he did with his place, what can Denis boast off, he can only boast with your money... I don't like him...I keep saying that and I'm not sorry...

"You are a talkative, you only knows how to talk rubbish, did Kuria paid you to talk me into giving him a chance, you and Kuria are crazy, if you don't stop this your crazy attitude of hating Denis I will have no choice than to put you a side like he said, he said you are jealous and I'm beginning to see reasons with him, you have your James who works his ass off every day so that you can have your dream wedding and home, you silently wish James has everything that Denis had, well life is obviously is unfair to you, your James has only one car which he has being using for years now and you have being with him for so Long, you only learnt driving last year and I allow you to drive one of my cars, why are you still with James is there no fine or Richer man to date aside James maybe with a better Man in your life you will stop hating my Denis, and why don't you date Kuria, the way you hype him why not go to him, he is quiet better than James, ohh..you thought I don't know how to throw hate speech too, you thought I don't have things to hate about James but I allow you be because you both love each other which is most important why not be happy for me too, why do you keep hating Denis, look at Vanessa we aren't so close but she likes Denis, she's always around him happy, Denis likes her too that was why he chose her to be my chief brides maid in place of you, you are just so hateful human being, I hate you when you hate My Denis, My husband to be...

"You sound so pathetic Joda, I thought I was the talkative but here you are holding a record in sounding so broken, talk about James all you want, that man is hard working, and all we need is to gather enough money to have a beautiful home not wedding, My wedding will be on low key, is after the wedding that the real marriage starts, not a Big wedding, Kuria is into you not me, how much much can he possibly pay me, I didn't ask you to have feelings for him or kiss him, you hate to hear about him because he makes your heart Skip just mentioning his name, just admit it, I love James because he is a good person, he works for his money unlike Denis who squanders and spend your father's hard aimed money the way he likes, well...I will talk less on that before you ask me if is My father's money he is spending, another point you made, Vanessa is not me and I'm not Vanessa, don't compare us, you just hate the Truth, Denis is very stupid for saying I'm jealous of you, I know you for years now even before you start dating him, what exactly should I really be jealous off, is it Denis or your money, you, Denis and Vanessa are crazy, I hate him because he is a gold digger... He doesn't deserve you Joda, Denis is into you because of your money... I hate to see him manipulate you the way he do, go and tell him I said he is a big fool...he..

Just as she was about to say another thing I raised My hand to slap her but she was too fast and held My hand,

"Hahaha...I must have hit you at the right the spot... Don't ever raise a hand on me again or I will break your fingers, or have you forgotten I went to Karate school... Hahaha...don't mind me, I'm only joking, but don't raise a hand on me because I will he force to hit you back, i take violence of any kind very serious, I'm not Kuria, if you slap me Joda I will slap you back, what is wrong with you, I wish you have all this action when it comes to Denis, have you ever raised a finger on him before no matter what he does, the answer is obviously a no, you can't do that with him but you freely swing your hands freely on people's faces, why not try it with your Denis, let me be going before you break My Head, but I'm a phone call away, if you ever needs me please don't fair to call and I will come running, you are still my friend and will always be, I can't advise you wrongly Joda, I'm only looking out for your good and I Hope and pray you understand that someday... Bye for now, don't fair to call if you needs me around.

Is being three weeks I never bother to call her and she never bother to call too, she is a bad vibes around me and I don't need such, everything is set for the wedding, I have gotten My wedding gown, Vanessa is mostly around, all the ladies are set,everything is set, invitation is all sent out, is definitely going to be a big wedding, Denis is obviously happy just like me, I'm getting married to the love of My life next week, this week is so slow, I wish it can run faster,

One of my girl came back from the market and said she saw Binta and James at Kuria's store, three of them where talking and ask about me and she told them I was fine,

After telling me that I felt like calling Binta to come around, I missed her and her talk, but she will come and start talking about how she hates Denis, I don't need anything negative now, Vanessa and others are doing great keeping me entertained but it can never be as Binta,

I'm looking forward to My day, my big day next week I just hope Binta will be there, all that mattes to me is that I'm happy but not so happy like i have expected to be, something is missing out somewhere, what could that be, i just hope this is a right decision so that I can prove Binta wrong.

Hope I'm not making a mistake, God please help me, I need all the help from you, I need My heart to be at peace, or is probably the tension from the whole wedding thing but I'm feeling empty.

JODA, Episode 7.

My wedding is in three days time, I'm all ready, well prepared For My big day, I'm getting married to the love of My life the only man I can't live without, the man that put smiles on face when I think of him, my hero, Denis My super Man, I just can't wait to be your wife.

I stood at my window facing the pool and watch as the Ladies swim, having lots of fun, I smiled to myself, and just picture how my big day Will be like with so many beautiful smiling faces surrounding me and my prince charming by my side

"Why not come outside and swim with the girls, are you alright...my soon to be wife..

It was Denis that held me from behind and gently spoke into my ear, I melted in his arms and my smiles was bold..

" I'm fine..my prince, my husband to be.. Is just three days from now we will be equally yoked together.. I can't wait my love... I can't wait to finally be your wife...

He kissed my cheeks and it felt so good, I thought of the day I saw him and Vanessa in the car and used the opportunity to ask him

"There was a day you drove in with Vanessa, and it took you both some time before stepping down from your car, then....I actually thought I saw both of you kiss before getting down...but I waved it off..maybe I was hallucinating...

" me kiss Vanessa... That's crazy thought... Yea..it maybe hallucination... Vanessa is your friend..I can't possibly cheat on you with your friend or anybody.. I love you Joda, relax your mind. Don't ever think of that... What do I wants in another that you don't have, you are my wife and will be mother of my cute kids, I love you so much Joda, my woman my everything.

I felt more at peace on hearing him say that, it was like a reassurance, I don't need any other prove that Denis was the man for me, I definitely knew I will prove Binta wrong, I really miss her and wish she's around me during this important moments of my life, I wish she will be around on My wedding day, maybe she's still angry with me that's why she have not call after the incident with her, and pride has held me from calling her, if I call her now she will feel I can't do without her and will start saying thrash about my Denis, the Man of my dream, I don't need that. I love Denis so much and I hate to hear anything negative about him, I know Denis can't cheat on me, if he does that.. I may not survive it, it will break me into pieces, and I know as he has reassured me that he will never do that, and I believed him, I know father will be so proud of my choice of man, I wish he was alive to hand me over to my hero, my Joy, the love of my life.

Today is the day, the days crawled so slow but we finally arrived here, the day I have looked forward to, as I walk down to meet my Denis who was standing at the alter waiting with the officiating priest, Vanessa was cleaning an invisible heat from My face, discomforting me with her constant adjusting and dapping my face with handkerchief, I whisper to her ear to take it easy, she smiled and nodded, this is when I so much wish it was Binta, Binta know what to do and does not over do things, the only thing she does excessively is talk, which can be entertaining sometime, and annoying too.

I Smile, my heart is filled with Joy as I walk down to my Denis who was also smiling too, he looked from me to Vanessa, I hated that I needed him to focus on me, not my friend, Vanessa, or was Vanessa looking more pretty than i do? but I was his bride not my bride's maid, I Smile despites all the thought going through my head as I urged him to look at me, which he later focused on me but glances towards Vanessa Once in a while she stood beside me smiling and looking at Denis as if she was the bride,

maybe I was becoming over jealous what is wrong if he looks at my friend, I waved the negative thoughts off my head,

It came to the time when the priest asked his usual question, the one that reminds me of the dream I ones had, "is there anyone who will not wants this couple to become husband and wife should speak now..."

I become scared... I scanned through the faces, they were all smiling faces unlike the ones from my dream. Everywhere fell silent just few murmur, I imagine my father standing up and moving towards me like a wind, but nobody stood up, I Wonder if binta really came, as I stand there scanning faces with my eyes. I saw Binta, she wasn't alone, she

was with James and Kuria was sitting beside James, my heart skipped as I saw him, he was looking so handsome in his gray suit and tie he noticed i was looking at him and smile, I quickly turn my face to Denis and took a deep breath and relaxed,
After all the long sermon we got married, as I walk down the aisle with Denis I saw Binta who was also standing among the crowds, she flashed me a fake smile, I knew that smile wasn't from her heart, I know her like my palm but I smiled back both to James and Kuria before going out with my husband, lots of congratulations where said, pictures taking after all the long ceremony it finally came to an end,
I'm happy I married the love if my life, Denis is the man of my dream,
I hope to have a fairy tale life like i have always wanted with Denis, let's see what after marriage will look like for me.

JODA, Episode 8.

"So we have being married for four months now, when will you finally change my name from the company's general manager to director, and also your father's other assets when am I going to be the sole owner because I'm legally your husband and you are under me and also under my roof...I owns you now Joda... So you will have to do according to My biddings... I dictate for you now and I'm your Lord...so what your father had before he died was given to you and now that you are married what you you have is equally mine... You can no longer claim anything as yours because you have a husband that is Lord over you... And if you disagree with me it will only mean that you are not a submissive wife but stubborn wife and I hate women who are never submissive to their husband, it means you choose your wealth over your husband, it also means you never love me like you claimed, I really need to be the Head over you and that includes everything your father Left for you, I want you to start now, call your lawyer let him start processing the papers I really need to know My stand darling, and I need to know it quick, I can't be intimidated by your money, is not right at all... I endured earlier because I wasn't yet married to you but now that I am I need things to change as soon as possible... If you truly see me as your crown, your glory, your love and your husband and also the father of our unborn children... And that reminds me, you also need to be pregnant as quick as you can, so that we can start making babies, this is the fourth month of being married, no sign of pregnancy you really need to visit your doctor again, he may prescribe something for you, because I don't want delay in having children, do the needful and come to me when you have something positive to say... I hate disobedience.. You are under My roof remember that Joda...

"Why so much in a haste to take over everything my father entrusted to me...I'm not under your roof Denis, this house was built by my father and was handed over to me...

" why do you have chicken brain... Or is there no sense left in your skull Joda... I'm sorry if you feel insulted but you just insulted me by reminding me that the House was built by your father, which automatically makes you the owner after his death.. You handed this House over to me before we got married, when I constantly ask you to do so, it took you so Long before you finally decided to call your lawyer who processed all the necessary document making me the real owner of this house...have you forgotten...

"No..I haven't.. But is still My father who built it, his hard sweat built this place and many others, despite the house is yours I'm not dragging it with you but acknowledge him...give him some respect and stop trying to take over everything he owns as yours, we are still very new in this marriage... So why the rush... My money is equally yours Denis, stop trying to be hard on me.. Knowing how much I cherish you, let's enjoy our marriage first before we start talking about property and money... Everything will eventually fall into place with time...please don't start this now is too early..I will see My doctor as you suggest concerning making babies, but relax My love let's be happy together, is too early to be having issue over irrelevant things....

After the quarrel with Denis I wasn't happy, how can he ask me to hand him all my father laboured for when he was alive, how could he even be saying that when we are just few months in to the marriage, talking about getting pregnant, I planned conceiving immediately after marriage he also wanted that too, but it hasn't worked as plan, it hasn't being easy for me but he is really making me to feel bad over changing his name to the assets, I know he loves me but what has gotten into him of recent, is it possible that Binta was right all along about the reason Denis got married to me, no it can't be. Is not possible, I love him and I know he also loves me too,

As the days goes I began to notice that I sleep too much, usually I love taking BlackBerry juice even before I sleep, my girls serve me the juice every evening before sleeping, but recently Denis sometimes brings the drink to me in the room, I'm always happy when he does that it looks so romantic, he sometimes send Vanessa to bring the drink, she is always full of smile and friendly as she does that, Vanessa has being shuffling from her place to mine, she sometimes comes to spend the weekend, the house was big and I didn't have any problem with her staying over but with time it becomes annoying because Denis will rather spent time gisting with her than having time for me, I'm always jealous when I see both of them laughing and talking, sometime if I join them I will feel like a stranger in there means, because they will change topic and start talking about some other boring thing that I hate, I wanted Vanessa to go and stop coming over more often as if she owns the House,

sometimes I think I'm over reacting or being too jealous because I wanted Denis all to my self, but I love Denis and I love it when he talks with me like he does with Vanessa,

Now in the aspect of the juice, I started noticing that I over sleeps anything Denis or Vanessa serves me, I will sleep from 7pm to the following day, 8am. It was unusual,

I called My doctor and told him he said i should come over that I'm probably pregnant but on

getting there it wasn't pregnancy, I wasn't pregnant but he said he noticed some hard drugs on my system, I told him I don't take hard drugs except what he prescribes, he asked me to watch my intakes, no damage was done yet but more of the sleeping substances would have caused a huge damage to my body system, I thanked him and Left.
I drove to Binta's place on my way home,
Someone have being putting hard substance in my food or drink which causes me to sleep like that, something is definitely wrong somewhere, I know it can't be my Denis, is probably Vanessa, why will she do that, i don't trust that girl not even her friendship, she is very cunning, maybe she want to take my Denis away, what if she's innocent,
what if....my head was full with "what if" I needed to talk to someone and Binta is the only friend I can trust, although we haven't being close like we use to after My wedding but she remain my bestie, I don't agree with everything she's says, but she has being a good friend to me and I can't just discard her because she doesn't like my husband, Denis doesn't like her too so they are even with each other.
A lot of things running through my mind as I drove down to Binta's house After doing a little shopping for her, maybe I can bribe her into forgiving me, i know she will never say no to her favorite stuffs,
I wanted to pay her a surprise visit and to apologise for bring a bad friend, I got her lots of things, including the food she loves, dresses, hand bag and shoes, but she wasn't around, I was told she went out with James who came to pick her up that evening,

I dropped all the things I got for her with her people at home before driving out to look for her at the only place that came to my mind
Kuria's place.

JODA, Episode 9

I double tap at the door, the house was quiet, maybe there's nobody at home, I tapped again for the last time no responds, as I was about to turn and start going the door swings open, Kuria was looking all fresh, he smells of alo vera soap, he was on Jean shot and a Lakers singlet,
He looks surprise to see me, I smiled and he smiled back
"What are you doing here Joda... Mmmh.. I'm surprise to see you, hope everything is alright.. Are you okay... How's your husband... Do you came with your friend Binta...oh..my bad.. Please forgive my manners... Come inside...
I wanted to decline the invitation to go in because of what happened the last time but the invitation was tempting and I stepped into his warm house...I really love his place.. Before he could even offer me a seat I have already Sat down, he sat in another chair
" I was just getting off from the bathroom when I heard a knock, I quickly rush up and dress before coming to the door, my teenage boy that stays with me has gone to school,
"A teenage boy... I thought you stay alone here?

" no...Jude is the little boy that has being staying with me for almost six years,there are two of them, Jude and Mera, Mera is a girl she's fifteen now, i also took her from the Street, she was just 9 years then and Jude was so little, looking malnourished when I picked him from the street, homeless little beggar, they don't have parents so I have being taking Care of them since then till date and they are turning out fine.. If school is on holiday that's only when you will see them, Mera is in girls boarding school and will soon be done with high school, Jude is just thirteen, they are doing good...and I feel so proud when I check their results, you will get to meet them someday...so what can I offer you... What of your friend Binta, the last time I asked her of you she said you are happily living the live you have always wanted and she's no More important... She sound so worried about you whenever I ask of you... She comes around with her Man, James sometimes... I love having and hosting them, Binta is a nice person and she cares about you More than you can imagine... And me too Joda, So what can I offer you please, I have different types of smoothy, and fruit juice, so what or do you want to serve yourself...
"Aaah...I'm fine Kuria, thanks, I thought I could find Binta here...i will be on My way thank you For your time..I will call her on phone...
In stead of standing up and go Sat there as if my buttocks is super glued to the chair, he sat there looking at me before saying
" Joda, Mumm.. I...I..please come around sometime, I'm still your friend, forgive me for what happen the last time, it will never happen again, and I

respect ladies a lot both married and single and I'm really sorry My feelings exploded, I couldn't get hold of it, unlike me but I promise it won't happen again, don't be scared of me, if you are not comfortable coming alone then come with somebody, Binta or anybody, even your husband... Please..

"Yeah, me too.. I'm also sorry for hitting you...but is all in the past now, I will be going now... My husband will be expecting me back... Please I will give you a call on when to start the interior deco, I haven't forgotten but I'm yet to speak with my hubby about it..

We were quite for sometime as we look at each other shyly, the temperature in the cold room was turning hot again, I started wondering what is it with this Kuria that makes my heart beat so fast despite I'm married to Denis the only man I love but Kuria confuses my feelings, I don't know how to define what exactly I feel for Kuria, it could be just be a mere attraction, deep down i knew there's more to it, i quickly stood up and went straight to the door, as I said within myself, " devil not today " you can't tempt me with Kuria again, I'm a married Woman...

he walked behind me as I open the door, I saw Binta coming down from James car, they both came to Kuria's place and was shock to see me there, before they could say anything I quickly started talking before they will assume the worst of me or Kuria,

Binta looked at me and didn't smile back as i smile to her, instead she held my hand like a child and drag me in side Kuria's house, leaving the men outside, as we were out of sight she asked me to start talking why I'm looking for her after I almost fought her because of Denis, she said it with a mean face, she asked if anyone hurts me and I told her about the sleeping dose and Denis constant threat over property and the rest, she swung into action and said I should install a CCTV camera in the house, all over the house and I should do it when there's nobody in the House, so that we can catch the culprit, I took the advice, because I need all the advise I can get now, she said first thing first, let's handle the issue with the sleeping dose in My juice, she told me not to take the drink when I'm served, rather I should find away to throw it off in to My toilet and make them believe I drank it, then I should just pretend to be asleep as usual and see what happens next.

I took Binta's advice this time be cause she began to sound right to me, i know I can always count on her, normally I plan to start taking My juice and food by myself, I can't trust anybody again in that house except my Denis, but Binta was right when she ask me to pretend to be asleep, acting as if the drink I took was having effects on me,

as evening approached I told my girls to get my drink to my room as usual, i said it in the presence of Denis and Vanessa who were sitting close by, i went back to My room and waited, after sometime Vanessa came with the tray containing the juice, so i was served the drink by Vanessa who was filled with mischievous smile, I smiled back to her while also saying My thanks, she sat with me and we talked for sometime before she left, she urged me to take My cold drink before it gets hot and I told her I will like it hot today, she said okay before finally leaving my room, when I was sure she was gone I quickly Rush to My toilet and pour the drink before flushing it off, I returned back to bed, and Vanessa later came again and ask if I need More I said I was fine with the one I have taken already, she flashed a smile before leaving with the tray and cup,

I later lay down and pretend to be asleep, she came and wave her hand to my face, to make sure I was deeply as sleep, this looks like a normal practice for her, she whispered to somebody who was close by, "she has passed out", and the voice that replies her "very good" was Denis, I was shock and become more troubled, what can Denis be planning with Vanessa that they have to drug me to achieve, oh my God...

I silently lay there like dead log...the next unbelievable thing happen which almost makes me to break out of the pretense but I stayed put Binta has warned me never to stand up no matter what I see or hear and i did exactly that,

but I so much wish I was already dead, I wish I can Even boast out crying as they went about their plan unknown to them I was fully awake.

JODA, Episode 10

"You know I truly love you Van, what is the problem today...are you mad at me..I'm sorry..what is the problem...

" I warned you not to touch her yesterday you still went ahead, and I didn't enjoy you the way I suppose to...
"C'mon van, I thought i have already said I was sorry, I can't avoid touching her,Joda is My Wife for now, we both got plan and I want her to take in, once she conceived I Will stop touching her, a Baby on her will break her down and perfect our plans, I know what I'm doing my love, just give me time, gradually, I'm not rushing up things please allowed me to take My time, you are the only one I love, you know that, my feelings for you can't be compared with what i have for Joda, I married her for a reason which you are also aware, ones I perfect everything, we will be together forever, please let's Work together in this, I need you close by, that's why I always hush her whenever she comes up with you going back to your place or my closeness with you, you matter most to me than anything in the world, I love you so much van...please kiss me..please...stop turning your face..I don't like it I needs you van..
" so is this how we will be drugging her every night to be able to be together, we have to drug her first, so that we can have enough time for ourselves.. I want to have you all to my self, as much as I agree to this marriage plans I'm beginning to regret it, because without her passing out we can't be together, Denis put your self in my shoes how will you feel if you are the one..is not fair on me...I hate to share, and the imbecile Joda doesn't really like me, she prefers her Binta friend, but I notice she's beginning to trust me and when I engage her into a conversation she seems to enjoy it, first thing first I

have won her trust...gradually we will win over everything... But I wish me and you will go over to my place or lodge in a hotel so that we can have enough time for ourselves...

"Van, I can't take any chance please, I don't want to be implicated, I'm trying to play safe and be very careful, Joda is deeply in love with me, and she does whatever I ask of her, she's naive and stupid, so I try to make her believe I love her Even though when I'm with her all I think about is you...just you van... I so much wish everything is ready for me and you to be together but is going to take time, just a little more patient and we will both celebrate...please My love..

I started hearing there dirty mouth sound as they kiss, I was still lying down like a log of wood without moving listening to them and sometime opening my eyes small to glance at there wretched and ugly faces as they talk, my heart beat was sounding like a drum to My ears, I was frozen dead, hot tears suddenly drop down from my face with the way I was lying down it won't be notice, another hot tears follow, heavy tears gathered in My eyes, I tried to blink it back but it rushed down like tap water, I was hurting, broken and troubled, everything sound like a dream but I was fully awake, how can this be, what did i do wrong, i still love Denis how could he do this, whaaat, oh my God, I wanted them to carry their cheating selves to another room, this is my room, there's several rooms they can do there shit, I didn't want to hear again, My ears where filled up, I was tired of hearing them, I became scared of what they will

say next, I don't want to hear the one that will finally kill me,
Cough held My thought, I desperately wish to cough out, but I held it as it stored up in My throat, one of them threw something to My face, I gradually opened my eyes little and it was Vanessa's bra, I looked at them, hot romance was really going on, I quickly shot My eyes, I will never forget the picture of both of them, when I couldn't bear it any longer, I was feeling choked up, I made a sound, and surprisingly coughed out, my eyes was still shot as I stretched My body, I pretend to be having night mare..
"Oh my God is she awake..she can't Wake up, I double dose her, I poured all the last content, making it a double dose, she wasn't Even suppose to make a noise until tomorrow, something is wrong Denis, check if she's awake, please remove my bra from her, I'm scared of getting close, she looks shrived unlike other days..please take off my undies from her face Denis..
" relax van, she's asleep, she can't possibly be awake, she drank all the content, but don't overdose her next time, put the normal quantity, you will buy another one tomorrow, don't panic my love, the over dose is taking effect on her, is stronger than the normal, please next time put the normal dose.. Let me get your bra so that we can move to another room..
He collected the bra and I gently opened my right eyes that I covered with my hands and saw Vanessa's dangling breast as she stood trying to dress up, I covered my eyes back, Denis called my name severally and Even shakes my body just to

assure Vanessa that I wasn't awake, but the over dose was taking effect on me, when she was calm Denis kissed her before they moved out, closing the door behind them as they left, I breathed a sigh of relief, I finally opened My eyes, I wept bitterly, I wept uncontrollable, silent weeping, I couldn't sleep, I was scared to sleep, I kept on watching the wall clock until it finally chipped 6am, I was still lying down when Denis came in and lay down beside me, pretending as if he spent the night with me,

When my wall clock chirped 6:30am, I stretched and opened my eyes, he was laying down looking up the ceiling, he turned and greeted me with a smile, and try to draw me close to him, just as usual, I shrugged and smile, and stood up, he came to hold me from behind kissing My neck, I gently pushed him off and entered the bathroom,

I was trying to maintain my cool, I so much wanted to bounce on him, tear him into pieces, burn down the house and anyone in it, I so much wanted to kill him and Vanessa but wisdom kept me calm, I got to be wise and act foolish to them, lets play this game, I love games and this game with Denis and Vanessa will be an interesting one, and I'm fully in, Denis is my husband, the love of My live, I gave it all to him and he thrashed me like a dirt, I will play this game well with them, thank God for Binta's advice,

Before I will quickly melt in his arms ones he touched me and I know he will be surprise that I resist him, how could Denis, I trusted him, my father also trusted him, how could he, proudly be cheating on me with my so-called friend,

First of all I will so cheat on him, I will frustrate him in this life that he will regret coming into my life to mess up, I know Who to use to cheat on him,
I quickly dress up, he has already slept off,
I see why he sleeps every morning, after having all night with Vanessa he will come to me in the morning, double portion for him, hmmm, he actually thoughts he was smart, let's see what happens
I dressed up and left that morning, I drove straight to Kuria's place that morning, I Will do exactly what my body has being wanting to do all this while, revenge is sweet
I will do it and rub it on Denis face,
I drove angrily to Kuria's place.

JODA, Episode 11.

I drove to Kuria's place that morning, i saw school bus parked outside his gate, but nothing was important to me than what I so much wanted to do, I ran up to to his front door, I knocked hard and he opened within second, he looked shocked to see me that morning but I wasn't thinking straight, I pounce on him like a prey, I started kissing and offing my cloths, asking him to make love to me, he was still shock as he takeoff his face from me, he tried to push me away still asking me to calm down, but I don't want to he calm, I wanted Kuria, I wanted him so much as I kept moving close to him as he steps back, my top blouse was already on the floor, it was remaining my bra and my jean trouser, but Kuria was resisting me,

"Joda...Joda please stop this and put on your cloth, Joda stop... Please, what happened... What's wrong... Talk to me... Please Wear......put your top back on... Stop

" I thought you wanted me, why are you running from me, I want you Kuria, stop pushing me away, please... I need you...please make lo...

"Uncle Kuria.. Is everything okay...is she alright?

I quickly turned and saw this cute teenage boy in his uniform and school bag hanging on one of his shoulder, he was standing on the wooden stairs that Kuria built.. He looks so confuse and looked from me to Kuria...I gently picked up my top on the floor and wore back without shame,

" hey Jude.. You are set for school... That's good... Pick up your lunch pack on the dining table, and run up because your school bus is waiting For you outside.. Yea, she's fine, she's my friend, her name is Joda, I will introduce you properly to her when she's in a better mood but run up now, be good my boy,

"Thanks uncle Kuria, see you after school.

Jude looked at me again, I wasn't in the mood to smile so I looked away, he ran out, Kuria took me to a seat and I quietly sat down, I need to make Kuria to do this with me, but he was trying very hard to resist me, I thought of plans

" Joda what is the problem, my boy was around and he doesn't suppose to see this drama, he is a teenager, and I'm trying to guide him through.. I don't want him misunderstanding this whole thing, teenage mind can work faster than you think, and what exactly happened... Talk to me, you can't drive down this early morning to my place just to ask me to... Hmmm this is crazy... I'm sorry Joda... But what exactly is going on,

"I'm sorry, i forgot you have a teenager around, I wasn't thinking.. I...i ...is just crazy Kuria, you won't understand... I had a fight with my husband and I needed to desperately talk to somebody, hmmm... I thought you actually felt the same way I have being feeling since we had that kiss, all I think about is you...Even when I'm with my husband...you occupied my mind... I...think I'm... Never mind...

I looked at his face, the trick was working, I smiled in my mind... Today with the way I wanted a revenge, with the way I desperately wanted to cheat on Denis I can't give up, I liked Kuria and I'm sorry for making him do this but it need to be done... I didn't want to talk to Binta because she will have some other plans outside this but I need to do this on my own, I know she will even be proud of me

" say it Joda.. You are in love with me? Isn't it, but you are a married woman, you are married, I promise you what happened the last time won't happen again, I can't do that because it won't be fair to your husband cheating on him...and I know you equally love him... From the very first time I saw you I have loved you Joda, but I kept my self in check because you were engage to be married and you will never be mine, and when we finally kissed back then I wanted to pour all the stored up feeling I have on you, i regretted it, and i watch you walk down to be married I started wishing I was the man getting married to you, my heart still beat For you even at this moment, but is a waste of time because you belong to somebody, you are the only Woman that melt my ego, and brings me to my feet any time I'm around you or I think of you, you got My heart right from the first day...I love you so much Joda but you can never be mine, and that's the fact and i can't tell you to leave your husband for me, God forbids if I ever do such a wicked thing, I will some day get somebody whom i will love with my life, and who will love me in return because I want to have a big family, and a happy one, I came from a broken home, I want something different and beautiful, I will never be a partaker in destroying another Man's own home because of my selfishness, go back home Joda, before your husband starts looking for you, I hate to see couples fight or unhappy, go home and sort out with him...he is your husband and will always be, if you don't love him or he doesn't love you you two won't be together... I'm always here if you want to talk but please come with Binta or somebody, is difficult sometimes having you alone with me, I must say the truth.. Joda, but all the same I'm always here for you, just go home, is too early for you to be out...

I Sat there not making a move, I intend to achieved my aim before going anywhere, on seeing I wasn't ready to go he wanted to call Binta to come over but I begged him not to, he breathed deeply before standing up to make some breakfast for me but i told him i wasn't hungry, he went to his kitchen anyway I later stood up and follow, a he bent over making scrambled egg, I put my hand under his shirt, holding him, he moan and turned trying to takeoff my hands, begging men to stop it, I did it even More since i know I'm difficult For him to resist me, I took my hands up his body and grabbed his breasts, I was good at what I do, he moaned again and pushed me off, he flee like the story of Joseph and potiphar's Wife in the Bible, I Sat where he pushed me, when he returned back to the kitchen he helped me stand, and apologised, he said I should be going or he will leave the House, I knew he wanted me but he was trying so hard to resist me, and I was working so hard to get him down, as he held me and talk I kissed him hard on the mouth, he tried to pull off but I held on tight, he struggled a bit before relaxing, I finally won, the next thing followed as we offed our cloths,I ask him to take me to his bedroom and he lifted me into his arm and carried me up there

After the whole thing I felt so good and he felt so broken, so later I said

"I enjoyed you more than My cheating husband, this is his revenge for cheating on me with my friend...

Kuria looked at me as if I said the wildest thing

" your husband slept with your friend, Binta?

"Not Binta, he slept with Vanessa, they are lovers, the idiot slept with my so called friend Vanessa, the girl that was my chief brides maid during my wedding, I caught them red handed, they usually drugged me just to do it...and I plan to cheat on him too,

" whaaaat, Joda.. God...so what we just did was only because of revenge, just because you wanted to cheat on your husband you came to me, how stupid can I be....jeeeeez...why didn't you tell me what you had in mind. Why tell me now that the deed is done... Why joda... Why do you hurt me this way, i felt terrible Already giving in to this, but with this realization I don't known if i can forgive my self, you manipulated me just to achieved your plans it wasn't Even because you have feeling for me..oh noooooo....I'm the because fool to have ... It felt like I took advantage of you Joda, you shouldn't have done this to me I truly love you...so much. That pushing you off and running felt like a knife was on my throat, ooh Joda....

His face was ashen, he looks as if he wanted to cry as he asked me to leave immediately, I try to apologise is not exactly what he thinks but he shouted and told me to leave,

by this time he was actually crying, I felt broken too seeing his tears, he actually tried to resisting me but i implore different tactics just to get him down, I felt so ashamed of myself as I walked out, I hated my self for making such a grown man to actually cry,

I drove home, and didn't come down from my car immediately as I got home, it wasn't the picture of Vanessa and Denis on my head again, it was that of Kuria, shameless regretting his action as tears pours from his eyes, if I hard known it will result to this I would have kept quiet and just do it and leave him in peace, i try getting My phone to call Binta, I couldn't find it, I have forgotten it at Kuria's place,

When I finally went upstairs to my room, Denis came to ask me where I have being but I didn't reply him, I was boiling on seeing his stupid face, as he came to hold me I gave him a double heavy slap, he held his face in shock, I started raining heavy causes on him, I released all my anger on him, but I never mentioned about me knowing his plan with Vanessa or about the drugs, I never mentioned last night to him I just caused and fight as he tried to hold me to himself, comforting me and asking me what happened,

Denis made me to hurt Kuria and I will never forgive him,

as he held me in his arm I poured out all the tears I have held back, he was acting all nice as he tried to wipe my tears, I slapped off his hand,

I'm actually done with foolishness, I really needs to talk to Binta probably she can help me beg Kuria to forgive me for manipulating and using him like Denis did to me

This is My wrong, I will Right it, this is my story and it must not end sadly for me,

JODA, Episode 12.

"What is Vanessa still doing here, the wedding has being over for months now, what is she still in my house doing...she is not my close friend, and i don't need her for anything, she have a place of her own...I only allowed her to best me doing the wedding because you wanted her and not Binta... So why is she still here... Coming and going as she likes...is there something you aren't telling me. Because I'm not blind to see the way two of you acts around me and in this house...Tell me what I need to know Denis because I'm tired of this whole shit...

" are you in any way accusing me of having something with Vanessa... This house is equally mine, and i can't cheat on you Joda I have already assured you that before now, How can you even be so cruel to van..she likes you and wanted to stay around as a friend.. There's enough rooms in this house that can take up to 20 people, or Even More, can you sleep in all the rooms at ones, Binta your friend is shrewd and she hates me as much as I do...Binta has a bad influence on you...van adores you.. Why don't you like her..

"Van...really Denis... Van...is that your new name for her now...because to my knowledge you calls her Vanessa... Stop lying, you look so stupid when you lie like this... I actually saw you kiss her inside that car which you denied when i confronted you, I saw you look at her on my wedding day, instead of me, the signs has being there but I was such a fool in love to even understand, guilt is written all over you and you Smell of it... Why do you have to use me to cover up...knowing well we are not close, you wanted her close by, I'm not a fool Denis..

" Joda please stop it... I don't have anything with Vanessa..you are My wife.. I assure you she will leave as soon as this discussion is over...I'm just close to her because she is a nice person...and she likes us...I love you Joda... Stop assuming the worst of me..

I looked at the face of a master liar, if not I caught them red handed during the night they thought they succeeded in drugging me..if not I saw and hard everything I would have believed him but I had a plan for both of them. I pretend like i believed him.. I need them to be caught in the act together..

"Okay, she can stay, I believe you.. Is just that I will so much hate it if you cheats on me...let her stay.. I'm cool my love...I'm sorry for doubting you...

He smile so broadly, and tried to hold me but I dodged it, the idiots doesn't know what is coming for them.. Let's play this game,

I stop the intimacy with Denis, whenever he ask or try to force himself on me I push him off and threatens him, he constantly reminds me of being my husband and deserve to have me any time but I also remind him that a wife sometimes needs break, and my doctor said I should not have anything intimate with him for now so that the drugs I'm taking can clear my womb for a baby to enter when we finally do it.. He has no choice than to believe the lies,

I called Binta with my landline since i forgot my phone at kuria's place, she said she has being trying to call me i begged her to come over, Denis left very early in the morning and Vanessa Left after an hour, my girls are also out of the house, she said she was coming over

After Thirty minutes she came in, when we were together, she opened her hand bag and brought out my phone

"My phone, I forgot it at Kuria's place.. He gave it to you?

" he called me over and gave me the phone to return to you...Joda what did you do to that fine man.. He wasn't happy and refuse to say much.. He hasn't even gone out since yesterday and he is obviously not himself... He only asked me why are women so manipulative, they takes advantage of you if they finds out that a man loves them and can't say no to them.... Well I didn't understand where the question was coming from so I told him is not all women, he shakes his head and gave me the phone to give you, I urged him to talk but he said he was done talking, so I want to know exactly what happened Joda...tell me what's going on...

I told Binta everything that happened right from the house to Kuria's place, she listened without a word, after I was done she slapped My face and said I was foolish, I was shocked that she strikes me, I opened my eyes wide and asked her what has gotten into her,

acting like she was my mother, she asked why didn't I call her before rushing to Kuria's house to have sex with him in other to revenge Denis, Binta was scolding me like a child, well I needed it I felt stupid myself after the act with Kuria, after all the whole shouting she held my hands and said I need to be wise and do things right because two wrongs can never make a right, she asked what I achieved now after I made Kuria to go down with me, I left him shattered and full of regrets, he is a good person and he truly loved me, what I did was very unfair to him, she said all this drama could have being avoided if I had listened to her right from the beginning, I would have being more happy with the man who truly loves me, that is Kuria, than the one that is after my money and properties, Binta talks as if she was send to me to direct me on the right track,

After the talk we called the CCTV Office and sounded so urgent, they came and planted the cameras round the house and rooms, where nobody can ever imagine anything of such is there, they worked so fast and gave me a small iPad where I can be watching and recording everything going on in the house, I paid them off and they Left.

I was happy and scared too because I know unknown things may eventually unfold, but I was fit and ready, a trap has being set for the culprits.
Binta gave me more advice, one which is to act all friendly with them in the house and i should always lock my wardrobe where I have important thing and avoid Denis touching me, I needed to divorce him but first of all let's sees what he is up to. Finally I need to make amend with Kuria, I have to call him or go with Binta to ask him to forgive me, I know he will not like to see me alone, but deep down I felt so betrayed by Denis but I still love him.
I agreed to everything Binta said planned, i was following them accordingly, I must try not to mess anything up,
Everything was going on fine, I make my own food sometimes or watch them from my CCTV iPad prepare it, so I know when is safe or not safe to eat or drink, I also told Denis I needed a room to myself that period so that I can concentrate on my doctor tasks, he later agreed after much persuasion, so I lock my room whenever I intend to sleep just to feel safe in my own house because I began to see I wasn't all safe from the things I hear and watch from my CCTV iPad, my evidence was building up I needed more to nail him. I felt bad for Denis, the

man I love, but Binta said I should put my feelings aside so that I don't complicate things.
No day past that I don't think of Kuria and how to face him,
I suddenly started feeling sick every morning and evening, I feel like throwing up sometimes, so without wasting time I drove to My doctor's hospital,
After the check up he confirmed that i was 7weeks pregnant,
it was supposed to be a thing of Joy but I wasn't happy because I haven't being with Denis for weeks now, Kuria was the last Man I met and i have being so occupied that I never listen to my body changes,
Oh my God...I'm pregnant but not for my husband but for Kuria, but it was just ones, this can it be, Denis has being with me severally and I'm never pregnant, Kuria touched me once and I'm pregnant for him
I was so devastated as I called Binta who asked me to come over to her place so I drove down, I felt so confuse, it was a very wrong timing to be going through this. I felt so tired, is very hard to be a human with multiple worries.
What I'm I suppose to do, why now I was almost actualizing my plans.

JODA, Episode 13.

"Yeah, I'm very serious...I'm pregnant Binta...I'm so confuse..I don't know what to do now..I didn't plan to be pregnant now.. Not now when I'm almost actualizing my plans...I'm pregnant...7weeks gone already... Binta you aren't saying anything... I said I'm pregnant...

" I heard you the first time Joda, exactly what Denis wanted, well with a Baby on the way that will thwart plans for you... But all the same be strong, I didn't want you to marry that man and you finally did, now you are pregnant with his child, he will be so happy, slow down with the plan, things will still work out for your good... I wish I can happily say congrats to you Joda.. But I still don't like Denis but I will love you and that baby as if we came from one womb, Denis wanted to get you pregnant by all means so that he can tire you down, now he has succeeded, but you must not allow him to put you where you don't want to be because you are his wife or soon to be mother of his child, you are still going to divorce that guy, he was never the Man for you, any way congrats... I don't want to make you sad...

"The baby is not for Denis..

" funny you Joda... If the baby is not for Denis, your husband or soon to be ex...then who are you pregnant for... Holy spirit? I'm sorry... I'm not really joking because this is serious issue... How do you mean...?

"Is for... For Kuria... I'm pregnant for Kuria... He was the last Man I met...Binta...

" waaaaat...are you kidding me...oh my God... Joda.. You are really pregnant for Kuria...then big congratulation girl... So happy everything is turning out fine... Denis will definitely loose, he will loose every thing he acquired through you, he will loose you and he will loose your child because is not his, ooh that guy thought he was smart... He is the biggest loser of the century, we are gathering enough evidence on him... Oh mine I love this...Joda you don't need to be sad..is a thing of Joy... Get up let's pay Kuria a visit...I know you and Kuria have being avoiding each other.. Is high time you face him and apologise because when I see a good Man I will know...and Kuria is a nice person who hates to be hurt... And you actually bruised his ego, but it can be amended...and you will amend it with your self and by yourself... Get up baby girl... Smile, no more sad face because I got you...

"Binta...you don't understand... I still love Denis... I hate to watch him and Vanessa on my CCTV iPad... I stop watching because it hurts so much...I love him and he is still my husband...

" snap out of that.. Did he use jazz on you that after seeing and hearing how he plan to take over everything from you, dump you and have a better life with his Vanessa... You listened to everything they planned...you watch them have sex in your house...thinking you aren't aware.. They use to drug you to do it until you found out... What is it in him that you love... Tell me what you love about Denis... Are you crazy Joda... Or he bewitched you with love...I would have given you are slap so that your brain can reset in order...get up my friend...I know when you see Kuria you will forget about Denis... I'm ready to cure you of that stupid thing you call love...

We later drove down to Kuria's place..he wasn't at home, his car was at the garage, which means he was at his store, we knew he will be there since he isn't at home, we drove down to his vegetable shop,

We didn't see him but he was around in his office, he probably saw us from the CCTV in his office because immediately one of his staff Left to call him we saw him walking toward us, my stomach made a sound... My heart began to beat faster, I couldn't look at him fully on his face, suddenly I felt headache... I rob my forehead...Binta spoke as he met up with us

"Hey Kuria... How are you doing today... We were at your place earlier but got the sign that you will be

at the store... You look good as usual...

" yeah Binta... I'm good... Thanks... Joda...how... Are you... Is being a while I saw you... Hope you are okay...

I looked at his face and he smiled... He acts as if he wasn't angry with me... I replied him with a smile too that I was fine, he nodded his head before looking at Binta, I miss his fine smiling face... I missed everything about him...Binta was right when she said I will forget Denis ones I set my eyes on Kuria, the headache was coming with force... I moved close to a wall to relax, Binta told him I have something to Tell him, he said okay without really listening to Binta as he came to me and held my shoulder asking if I was alright I smiled, Binta replied him, she told him I was just tired... He suggest we go to his place and we Left, he collected my car keys and he drove us down.

When we got into his place, something nice filled my nose, it smells like food, Binta asked what exactly was the smell he said it was cake, Jude did

his birthday yesterday, so few of his friends came around and he made cake for them, that the remaining one was in his fridge, before Binta could ask for some he already got it for us, it looks so delicious, it was a fruity cake, I wanted some, i wanted binta to look at me so that i can give her sign to cut out some for me but she was busy loading the cake into her mouth, without a care, my stomach made another sound, i seriously wanted some but he was looking at me and I was shy to cut by myself, as if he noticed and got a disposable plates out and cut for me, allowing Binta to served herself, I wondered how he knew my thought, I couldn't even tell Binta because she may end up embarrassing me, Binta love food.
Kuria is good with what he does, a super good Cook and an interior deco Who runs a vegetable store, I envy him..I envy the woman he will get married to because she will have a super Man as husband, I silently wish i was his wife and not Denis wife, I thought of my baby, my heart began to beat faster, how do I even tell him he is the Father of my unborn child, how will he take the news, I looked at him and he was still looking at me and suddenly looked away, Binta was busy with cakes and drinks that I prayed for her silently so that it won't have a side effects on her, with her mouth Full she glanced towards me and winked at me, with cake crumbs scattered on her face, she looks so crazy that I boast out laughing, she' always feel at home whenever she's at Kuria's place, she act like is her house and Kuria likes her realness, as I laughed, she held her mouth and laugh too, the scenes looks so funny that Kuria joined in the laughter.

After she swallowed the thing in her mouth she stood up with another plate of cake with drink, she told Kuria that I have something to say to him, she stood up and walked out on us

The living room fell silent, Kuria who was sitting at the dining with me looked at me shyly before saying

"I missed you Joda.. So much...I'm Glad you came...how are you doing...

" I thought you didn't want to see me again after the last time... I'm really sorry Kuria... I didn't mean to take advantage of you...I know you were hurt...I'm so sorry...

"Yeah...me too, I was so hurt Joda... But later I started missing you, I wished I could just see your beautiful face again, is being more than a month.... Is all in the past Joda.. I'm Glad you came...how are you...

" thank you Kuria... I'm fine just having headache...

"Headache... I'm coming let me get you something, you will feel fine in a seconds..

He stood up and Left and returned with a glass of green content, and gave me to drink, I didn't want to take anything that will harm my baby, but i trust Kuria but I wanted to know if is safe for a pregnant woman,

" go ahead and drink it all, you act like you are scared, don't be, I will never hurt you joda...is herbal green tea, it will Stop the headache...

"I trust you Kuria...I..I...don't know if is safe for... me...if is safe for preg.....woman..... I'm... Pre....

The word got stock on My throat, I looked at him his face changed, I looked away, he gently turned my face to him

"You are pregnant... Uuuh....is nothing to be ashamed of, congratulation Joda... Your husband will be so happy... I'm also happy for you... Is called for celebration... Hmmm....how I wish I was your husband... I Will be extra joyful....that's crazy....take your drink is safe for you and your baby...
I love you joda... I still do...and will be here for you if you ever need me, is sound very stupid to hear that I'm in love with another Man's wife, I Will get my woman someday, love her with all my heart and she will give me children be cause I want a big happy family...relax Joda and take your drink... Is safe...
I smile and didn't know what to say him, I went close and kiss his forehead, I sat back and took the drink, he smiled expressing his white well set gaped teeth,
I wanted to be seeing him everyday because he is an antidote to my happiness, I love Kuria, he is truly a good man as Binta will say, some day i will muster courage to tell him he is the father if my Baby, today isn't the right time, i told him to come and starts the architecture work in my place and he agreed, atleast I will get to see him everyday,
I drove home with Binta and saw Denis, he bought so many beautiful bouquet Flowers for me, many gifts
I asked him what we are celebrating because today wasnt my birthday
He was so happy and was kissing me all over, he was full of joy as he said that the doctor called congratulating him, he said we are expecting a baby..

JODA, Episode 14.

"I knew you wanted to surprise me with the news when you get back so I decided to surprise you instead by getting your best Flowers and things you love, I'm so happy Joda, we will finally have the baby we have being anticipating for, doctor knew how we wanted this,that was why he called thinking you have already told me...I love you so such Joda... You are my beautiful wife and the mother of my child...

" Binta was sitting at one corner looking at us as Denis hugged me I face Binta who rolled her eyes and stick out her tongue for Denis who was backing her, I suddenly boasts out laughing as Binta made funny face to Denis, calling him a loser silently that only me saw and understand... I suddenly boast out laughing and Denis thought I was overjoyed over the baby news just as he was, he also joined in and laugh not knowing exactly why I'm laughing...he was actually laughing at his own foolishness without knowing

I felt so sorry for him because he is happy over another man's pregnancy...

Denis was so happy that he even ask me and Binta to dress up he was taking us out, it was very surprising because he was never a friend of Binta, we both said were tired maybe next time, he agreed and said he will go and buy whatever we want to eat For us...

We were already filled up from Kuria's place so I called him and asked him to relax we will have another day to celebrate,
Vanessa came, when she hard the news she came to congratulate me, Binta looked at me without a word, I thanked Vanessa, she stayed a little while before going, Binta boasts out laughing again, as she closes the door behind her, i looked through my CCTV iPad and saw her behind my door trying to eavesdrop on us, I showed Binta and she tiptoed to the door and forcefully pulled it open Vanessa fell on the floor like a bag of sand, Binta acted surprise and said "Vanessa didn't know you are relaxing on the door...thought you are already gone"
Vanessa frown before standing up and walking away, Binta shut the door and we started laughing again,
Binta stayed with me for three days before going, Denis was unable to come to me at night because of I told him I needed my friend to stay with me, he listen to whatever I say and does whatever I demand since he discovered about the pregnancy, even from My CCTV videos, he no longer touches Vanessa at night, which resulted to one of their silent quarrel in the mid night when they thought every one was asleep,
Binta has asked me to go and warn our family doctor over his unzipped mouth, he wasn't the one to pass the news to Denis but me and now Denis will not allow me to rest because of the Baby he thought is his,
Before Binta left I drove with her to the doctors place and cautioned him over letting my husband

know anything about me and the baby, he sincerely apologised and promise it won't happen again, Binta also warned me about having intimacy with my husband, she asked me to try and avoid it until my lawyer serves the divorce paper which will still take time because of my present condition, the truth is I don't know how Long I can avoid Denis,

I called Kuria and asked him when he was coming over, he agreed to come the following day I sent him my address

The following day he drove down in his brown SUV jeep, immediately I sighted his car driving towards my gate I knew he was the one, I already told the security to open gate for him and as I watched from my upstairs they quickly opened the gate for him and he drove in, I was already down stairs when he came into the House, Denis was around, Vanessa wasn't home, i have already told Denis about one of my friend who is into deco, coming to renovate our House and he quickly agreed and said I can have anything that makes me happy,

Denis was acting all Nice this period,

So I forgot myself and ran to Kuria throwing myself in to his arms, I knew he was surprise but he held me for sometime and quickly released me immediately Denis came down, they exchange pleasantries by handshakes, Denis came to where I stood and gently held my waist as he spoke with Kuria

"In few months time there will be an addition to our family... My beautiful wife is expecting a Baby and she wants everywhere to be renovated, she mentioned you are her good friend and also good at what you do, please decorate any design she chooses, money is not the problem, feel at home here because it Will make my wife happy, especially since you are her good friend, me I'm so Happy and her happiness is my top most priority...please feel at home here and eat or drink anything you so desired, take your time and do your job if it will take you months or weeks just take your time and give her exactly what she wants

Denis bent over and kissed me in front of Kuria Who stood watching and have to look away, I pulled back my face and frowned at him he quickly apologised with a smile and looked at Kuria before saying he loved me so much and couldn't get enough of me.

Kuria smiled and flashed his white teeth as he thanked Denis and me for the job, and for having him, he was acting all formal, I wish hr can look at me more but he was focusing on Denis and only glanced through me,

as we were about to move to show Kuria round the house Vanessa came in, she made a new hair and had this heavy make up on her face,after saying hello to me and Denis who was still holding me, she exclaimed shamelessly when she saw Kuria

"Wooow...what planet do you fall from...you looked like the god of mars, you are handsome... I'm not flirting, just saying the fact...

Kuria laughed and thanked her, Denis smiled and said

" you must be getting lots of compliments from ladies, with your body built, I know most ladies can't get pass fine Man like you... But people like you are mainly a play boy, they don't have or love one person...they are Casanovas, players that easily deceive women...

I immediately slapped Denis hand off me, he was embarrassing Kuria Who was just smiling without a word, Denis saw I was angry and quickly apologised, "

"Kuria please don't take offense, I said "people that have your kind of look" I didn't mean it to be offense, Joda I was only joking with him, I'm sorry if that offends you, Kuria my sincere apology,

Kuria smiled as usual and said no offense was taking, we showed him places, he wrote and Drew somethings in his working sheet,

After that Denis took me upstairs, Vanessa refuse to leave Kuria to work, she follows him wherever he goes, talking non stop, Kuria was only smiling as he worked without paying much attention to her,

As I was in the room with Denis my heart was where Kuria was, what if Vanessa seduced him, if I know I would not have ask him to come over and sending Vanessa out now Will be suspicious,

I was still thinking about Kuria when Denis came again thinking I'm angry with him and started apologizing,

He looked so innocent as he knelt down holding me, I allowed him to kiss me which led to another level, I still love Denis, and I love Kuria too, I'm carrying Kuria's child, he doesn't know yet,

Denis thought is his and have totally change to a good Man, deep down I love the man lying down beside me, I have always loved Denis, I don't even know how to stop, despites everything I have seen and heard from him, what I feel for Kuria is so different, I'm always happy being around him, for the first time in almost two months i finally lay with Denis, my mind was on Kuria as the whole thing went on,

Kuria came the following day, i didn't know when he left the previous day, denis purposely like kissing me where kuria can see us, Kuria is never comfortable when ever Denis start acting all lovey dovey around him, I pretended because I don't want to be suspected, Kuria always shows his discomfort when ever Denis is holding me,

is being two days Kuria started the decor thing, I watch him from a distance as he worked sometimes, it was difficult having him close yet I can't get close, because this days Denis refuse to leave my side and Vanessa always want to be where Kuria is,

Kuria does not really pay attentions to Vanessa, I started feeling bad about Kuria and Vanessa, what if Vanessa succeeded in seducing him,

many things went through my mind as Kuria drove in one day, it was a Saturday he came with Jude

Denis wasn't home, Vanessa was swimming, my girls are busy in the kitchen, I allowed Kuria to start work before i went down, Jude greeted me as he saw me, Kuria looked at me and pulled off his gloves, he wasn't happy as he said he may not be able to continue the work, reasons Best known to him, I pleaded with him not to do that, he asked jude to get him something from the car, after the boy Left he said he couldn't Bear it anymore, watching my husband kiss and romance me in his front, he said it was a silent torture to him, he losses concentration because of that, as he saw

Jude approaching he kept quiet and he didn't say anything again,

he wore his gloves back and went back to work, he wasn't happy, if is just because of what Denis does, it wasn't really enough reason For him to decide to stop work like that, Denis is still my husband

I wanted to know why he isn't happy but I know he won't answer me, Vanessa came in wearing her swimming pant and bra, she used a pieces of scarf to tire her waist, she came to Kuria who didn't pay her attention, or turned to look at her, he was busy working,

I later left them, Vanessa followed me and asked me why Kuria doesn't like her, she said she really likes him and she begged me to talk to Kuria about her since he is my friend, I agreed just to dismiss her,

In the evening when Kuria was about going I saw Vanessa telling him to drop her off that she was going out, I watched from my room balcony as Kuria opened the passenger door for her as she suddenly kissed his cheeks Kuria's face was a mark of shock as he used his left-hand to clean his cheek and spoke to Vanessa silently. She frowned and nodded, kuria entered the car and drove off,

I felt so bitter, I was jealous that I wish I can tear Vanessa into pieces, but deep down I trusted Kuria but what Denis said about him do ring in my Head, kuria is not a player or Casanova, i know is not true, Kuria is hard working, he has being training two street kids for years now, and doing it happily, he is a people's person, Denis is only being threatened by him, Kuria is successful and good looking too,

Tomorrow was Sunday he won't be working I wish I can go over to his place but I can't,
I can't Tell Binta about me giving in to Denis, I know she will be mad but Denis is still my husband and I still feel something for him,
I can't confront Vanessa about Kuria and asking Binta to do that may attract questions,
I'm still in this act nobody must know what I'm up to except Binta,
But how do i Even tell Kuria that the baby I'm carrying is his,
How can I love and still hate Denis at same time, he seem to be acting all Nice and fully devoted to me, why now that I'm pregnant, when I have a bucket full of crabs about him,
Is it possible to love two people at same time because I love Kuria and I feel very bad when I see him with Vanessa,
Kuria won't be around tomorrow but I will talk to him when he comes on Monday, a lot of talk, I just hope nobody will be home except the securities so that I can have enough time
I waited For Kuria Monday he didn't come and I didn't see Vanessa either, on Tuesday Vanessa was around but later left, she was not happy, I didn't bother to ask why she looks so sad because she's non of my business, still no sign of Kuria,
I called him but no response, after Wednesday morning came and gone I drove down to his place, he was home, and opened the door as I knocked, I stepped in, he wasn't looking happy and I wasn't happy either, and I need to sort things out, today I made up my mind to tell him he is the father of my child, he deserved to know although I still have

double mind about telling him but I can't keep punishing myself, I truly love Kuria, or I'm probably confused.
I wish I can finally be happy with the man I truly love, I planned to get it done with Denis as soon as I can, but his recent behavior is what i don't even understand but I really need to be focus on the task before me, just as Binta will say.

JODA, Episode 15.

"I haven't seen you for some days, and I also called but no response, do you really want to stop the Work just like that...why are you upset..more reason I came...
" I'm fine Joda, I decide not to stop the job, I will come and continue ones the materials I ordered for arrive, I called they said they will deliver it tomorrow, so I wanted to wait until tomorrow before coming over, because I really need the wood materials, yeah..I missed your call I plan to return it later but forgot, sorry about that, I would have told you or your husband about the delay but you seem busy with him most time... Well never to worry I will continue your decors tomorrow...
He fell silent, and picked up his Biro and a note book, jotting something without really paying much attention to me, I sat opposite him, why is he acting so formal with me...
"Kuria, are you angry with me or with anyone, you look dull and you aren't even paying attention to me... What is the problem...

" I'm fine Joda, you have my ears, need to write this measurements down before I forgets it,

"Did Vanessa came down here, I mean did she visits you... Being seeing both of you... Back in the house though...and... She said she likes you.... Do you like her...

He looked at me fully, and smiled mischievously..before saying..

" Joda is that your way if pushing me off, pushing me to your friend.. I don't, I hate it when she acts like a harlot around me, I warned her about that the day she asked me to drop her off and she suddenly pecked me, I don't go around with every Lady, I got lot to do with my time, falling in love with you was never in my list this year, and don't think i go about falling for everyone, I'm better off than that, I'm planing to take off more Street kids off the Street, is going to be a big project and I have to work hard towards achieving that, I don't invite every body to my House... If you notice all the while you or Binta has being coming over if I was inviting everyday Lady that showed interest in me or I came across to this place you would have being meeting lots of them, i don't keep friends, I'm afraid to love the wrong person... I'm taking my time to get it right, Vanessa is a beautiful Lady but she is just like everyone out there... I don't just allow anybody into my life Joda, I fell for you from the first day I saw you, you even saw through me and flashed your engagement ring to My face.... Just to scare me off, I took precautions but I don't know how yo stop thinking about you or stop loving you even after you got married, I still don't, you know you are my weakness, I can't say no to you, I have really tried hard to take you off My mind but I just can't, and when your husband goes about kissing and holding you in my presence I felt like I was punched to the face, no matter how cool I appear physically i was seriously sweating inside, is driving me crazy, I know he is your husband and he is free to have you anywhere but can you please Tell him to keep bedroom things to the bedroom, your intimacy with him shouldn't be a problem to me if I could stop thinking or loving you but you are my weakness Joda, please for me to be able to do my job effectively I will need all the concentration I can get, I almost stop because of you last week, when I couldn't Bear it any longer, is as if my face or where I'm working was always the perfect place to kiss you, I'm only doing the job because of you Joda, I want you to be happy, stop allowing him to taunt me, tell him to keep private things private, I still don't know why he does that Or do you believed what your husband said about me... Is fine though, it doesn't matter because you are happily married and carrying his child, and he kept on rubbing the whole thing to My face...and now you are asking me if I like Vanessa...

"He is my husband Kuria, but not the father of my... My...I mean he only does that because he felt threatened by you, he just did that to show off, Vanessa was the Lady he had an affair with...

" so what is she still doing in your place, she had affair with your husband why is she feeling like is all normal and you are so cool, looking at what I witness in your place you seem so fine with that, and why are you still asking me if I like her...I seriously don't understand anything about you...

"I'm gathering an evidence about them, I'm planing to divor..... You won't understand Kuria, let's leave it like that...there's so many things I wish to tell you...but words fails me every time I open My mouth,

He moved to where I Sat, and sit beside me, he drew me close to his body, felt so relax lying in his arm, non of us said a word as we Sat quietly, he kissed my hair and relaxed his Head on the cushion while still holding me, we stayed that way for a very Long time until I felt sleepy and slept off in his arm

When he tapped me awake I discovered that i was in his bedroom covered with a duvet, he carried me down as I slept to his bed room, covered me up, he Sat besides me and smile,

he said is getting late I need to be on my way home before my husband start searching for me because he has being calling my line, Kuria also said he prepared a chicken soup for me while i slept, and packed it up, I thanked him and step down from his big bed to Wear my sandals, he grabbed My legs into his laps and wore them for me, I smiled and went down to take my chicken soup so that I can be going, it was already 8pm, I slept for two hours, if not that Kuria woke me up I would have still be sleeping,

As I got into my car he bent over and kissed my forehead, and said he will be driving behind me until I gets home, and he did, he drove one of his small car behind me wearing a face cap, until I got in to my estate, he turned and drove back.

Denis was pacing up and down when I got home, i just told him I was with Binta after which I visited the hospital for check up and he said I would have told him to drive me to wherever I was going or pick his call because he was worried, he said he will get me a driver and i told him I don't need any body driving me because I love driving my self

The next day Kuria's wooden materials for the interior decoration arrived, he came with 2 young boys, Who worked with him, they were his student, he was teaching them about the interior deco thing

He smiled at me when he saw me and asked if I rested well I smile back and thanked him for the soup he prepared for me because I really enjoyed it, Vanessa suddenly stopped coming over again, days turns into weeks, and months, kuria finished the deco and it was fantastic, so beautiful, I paid him but the returned back the money, I insisted but he refuse to collect a dime, I couldn't thank him enough for the perfect work he did, he said he Will be travelling out of the country to visit his Mom, which he does ones in a year and will spend just a month there. I hugged him and wished him a farewell, I Will Miss him a lot while he is gone.

Binta was mostly with me as my time to give birth drew near,

Denis has being so nice, that i don't bother to watch him again on my CCTV iPad,

he came back one day without his car, he came in a taxi sweating and acting as if he was in trouble, I became scared when he said he needed a very huge amount of money because he knocked down somebody with his car unknowingly and the police also ceased his car, because I was the only signatory to my father's company account, i told him the 10million that he was asking for was huge, it will cripple the account i can only give him 7.5million, he held me and begged me to give him the 10million he was requesting For if i truly love him and don't want to see him in jail, I was thinking so hard he can't be lying with this kind of stuff,

but taking such amount out will affect the account, I didn't know what to do because of the way he was acting I took my cheque book and signed 10million to him, after i handed him the cheque he kissed me and ran out,

After one week, he was always going out whenever he wants to make call, it was binta that Drew my attention to it, Binta asked me one day why Denis is always hiding and making call,

so i decided to watched him from my CCTV iPad and saw as he called somebody, I listened and heard him say to the person that she should wait for him there, he has gotten the money from me, and her cut will be 2million because he only collected 5million from me, the person argued with him that he collected More than that and he started swearing that he only collected 5million.

already the money has being transfered to his personal account, Binta wasn't aware of this, I didn't Tell anybody because I felt foolish after giving him such a huge amount, Binta wasn't around, there's was nobody to talk to, father Will be so disappointed in me if he was alive, I almost fainted because Denis used a false pretense to collect 10million, crippling my late father's account, this was the last straw for me, I Will get my lawyer and see if I can get my money back, I'm so done with Denis, is probably Vanessa he was planing with and I actually thoughts he has changed,

I'm calling my lawyer right away, I was shaking all over as I dialled Binta s number instead she will be equally disappointed but she will Tell me what to do, I don't want to make a rational decision that will backfire or have regrets but I needed to get my money back before is too late...

JODA, Episode 16.

Is Denis... He collected money from me with false pretense... He said he was in trouble and needed money, and he was to go to jail if he doesn't get the money... I was scared Binta with the way he was crying and sweating...so I wanted to reduce the amount he asked for but he insisted on the exact cash he asked for, he said if I truly love him I will do it...because I can't watch him go to jail... And I love him, I know you will be mad at me but I love Denis and as he pleaded I gave him the money...I use to tell him that my money was also his money...what is the use of the money when I can't use it to save him... And he has being acting like a changed person since the news of the pregnancy got to him... Lots of thought was going through my mind and I gave him the money... Binta... I believed Denis and signed the cheque for him...I just found out he wasn't in any trouble, after you told me he has being hiding to receive and make calls, I went through the CCTV iPad and there he was telling somebody he has collected the money from me and will give the person his/her own share, he even lied to the person whom I think is probably Vanessa, he didn't tell her the actual amount he collected from me... Binta...the sad part is that is my Dad's personal current account, that I'm only signatory to... I froze my dad's account Binta, I can't even explain how Denis got me into doing that but he really got me... I want my money back...I did the worst foolish thing, my father would have called me an illiterate fool, because I suppose to know better, I was trained to be smarter than that...I don't even know why I do lots of foolish things, things that i regrets later...I loved Denis and he knew I love him why will be hurting me deliberately, why... I deserve better than this... I thought he has changed... He has being super nice of recent... And I was beginning to fall in love all over again with him, I was beginning to trust him again... I stop watching him constantly on the CCTV, I thought he will never use something so serious as that to lie, he was sweating and crying... Denis deceived me, I don't totally blamed him...I shared in it because I acted so foolishly without thinking... I'm already 9 months and Will be welcoming my baby any moment from now.. I don't suppose to be going through things as serious as this... I hate Denis... No...no...I so much hate him for being s wolf in sheep clothing... For betraying my trust...I hate Denis for taking advantage of the love I have for him...I so much thank God he isn't the father of my child, For this thing he did...I will never accept him back into my life again, He is a fraudster, and he dupe me, but the thing is i was wide awake when I signed the cheque book, he will never go

Scot free... This is the last straw for me, that jail he said he didn't want to go that was why he needed the money...he will rot away in there...Denis will rot in prison, I will make sure of that... He has chewed More than he can swallow... I will tell him I'm not blinded in love anymore.. God...I hate Denis... Binta men... Men are terrible...

"Hey...is only your Denis that is terrible... My James is a good man and of course Kuria is an Angel... So your Denis is the only terrible person I know, calm down joda, remember your condition, don't tell Denis that the love you have for him is not blind... Show him... Prove it to him joda, I'm so tired if him manipulating you all the time, You are venting out venom and hating Denis now by the time he comes rubbing his hand on your back and acting like he was going to slump and die....by the time he comes begging you to forgive him...I won't be surprise if you later come telling me... "Binta, I have to forgive him...because he is my husband and i love him... Don't come telling me that Joda. Please be serious this time and mean it... I keep saying it, if you had listened to me when I told you not to marry that man, you would have save yourself from all this drama, you did not mention the amount Denis collected from you..or are you ashamed to say it...

I told Binta the amount she screamed, she stared at me with her eyes wide open and mouth open, and asked if i was charmed to have given Denis such a huge amount, it sounded so unbelievable to her, but we eventually planned, Binta calmed me down and said we will get the money from Denis, I called my lawyer, who said he was on his way the police,

before my lawyer with some police men could get down to my house Denis drove in, he was happy and Even got a set of bouquet of flowers for me, Binta gave me sign to play along until my lawyer arrive with the police men, but I was done playing along, i threw him the stupid flowers he gave to me, I asked him where he kept my money, he tried to play drama by acting as if he doesn't know what I was talking about, when I told him that the police was on their way to pick him up, he laughed and said it wasn't possible, my love for him will not allow me to hurt him, I laughed back and told him to watch out, as he was still talking the police siren blew, signifying that they are near by, he got scared and dialed something on his phone, I tried to get the phone from him but he pushed me off and i landed hard on a cushion, I started having contraction, as I screamed Binta rushed in, on seeing me in pain she turned to Denis who was still pressing his phone fast and gave him a heavy slap, Denis tried to slap but she dodged before kicking him hard on his manhood, Denis shouted in pain,
"Gold digger like you... You can lie to her and steal from her I won't be affected because she bargained for this but if you dare try to physically hurt her or lay a finger on her you Will have me to contend with, I will use my last blood to make sure you rot in hell, gold digger like you... Your cup has filled up with your sins, shameless fraudster that even dupe his own wife, I hate you Denis, and the hatred has even, but what I feel For you now is sympathy, foolish man...
Binta rushed to me and placed my leg on a table, as she was still doing that, Denis was saying, " Joda

you watched your Friend slap and insulted me, Binta you will regret ever raising your hand on me, he was still threatening when the police came in with my lawyer, because I was in a little pain Binta spoke with them, they handcuffed Denis who was saying is a family misunderstanding that does not require the police, he said that the Police wasn't suppose to be involve,

They ignored him one of the Police men took him away while others stayed behind with my lawyer, as I played the video to them, only the part Denis spoke with somebody about the money he collected from me, it was enough evidence that he collected money from me through false scheme,.

Binta told them not to mention anything about the CCTV camera to Denis, they later Left and Binta collected my car key and drove me to the hospital.

I was admitted in the hospital, and gave birth after one week, my daughter arrived by exactly 3am on a Saturday, she was flawless, so beautifully created,

Binta was with me all through the difficult moment even after I gave birth to my girl,

My lawyer said Denis was in jail but there was no money in his account, they checked all his account but found nothing but has agreed to pay me back my money, Denis told my lawyer that is family thing and no law is needed to resolve it, "she is still my wife and her money is equally mine" he will find means to borrow so that he can return back my money, he told the police men that he needed to go and see his wife and his baby girl,

my lawyer asked me what I wanted I told him to tell the police to release him, and after he returns the money he should served him a paper for

divorce, I finally made up my mind I was divorcing him,
Denis came back home, and went on his knee, begging me to forgive him, he said he was actually in trouble, he met some 419 men, who threatened him, they said if he doesn't get them such a huge amount of money because they knew my father was a rich Man when he was alive, according to him the 419 threatened to kill me and my unborn child if he doesn't bring the money, so he lied because he does not want me to get scared, he gave all the money to them, that the Police didn't find any money in his account because he has emptied his account to the 419ers and was koboless before coming to me, so I told him that I don't believe his story, all I needed was my money, he cried and pleaded that he doesn't have any money, I told him even if is half of the money he should bring it or he will be going back to jail, he said he will run around to see if he can borrow to give me, I told him I don't Care where he gets it from all I want was at least 5million, let me leave the remaining 5million for him and his stupid stories which I'm not sure if they are true or not,
It was a tough moments For me but my baby, Luella was my Joy, she has her fathers beautiful eyes, Kuria was already a father without Even knowing it.

JODA, Episode 17.

Denis later returned half of the money to me, and said he borrowed it because the fraudsters collected all the money from him, I didn't Care about his stories, i collected the money from him,
He was acting all beaten but I told him to stay away from me and my daughter, he argued with me that Luella was equally his daughter and I can't ask him to stay away from her, I told him I wanted divorce, he laughed and said I can't divorce him because I'm too soft and he knows I still love him, "if I can send you to jail to be tortured, Denis I'm capable of anything, you took my love for granted and did all manners of things, I'm done with you, you took my gentleness for granted Denis, you cheated and lied right under my nose...you are my mistake and I Will correct you,
" Joda, God bear me witness I never cheated on you, I never lied to you... I love you Joda, this period is a trying time for us and please let's Work together like one family to get pass it, Luella is the child God used to reveal that we are meant to be together, we are blessed with a child, I want to be in the live of my daughter, I want to watch her grow and I want to be a father she will grow to be proud of, Joda stop all this, how can you be using something as serious as divorce to Joke... I don't like that... I know I wronged you but I'm sorry...I have knelt down to beg you, you allowed them to take me jail and tortured me before asking them to release me, that was very cruel for somebody you claims to love, I know is Binta that is behind all this,

you are listening to that wicked fool, Binta is only jealous of you, stop allowing her to be close to you, she's good for nothing, you watched her slapped me and abused me without doing anything, Binta is only out to destroy our family and God will not allow her because I know love conquers all things...
He kept on talking I asked him to leave, I'm done with his cooked up lies and I mean it this time,
He later Left, I was watching him non stop on my iPad,
I later found out he transfered the money to Vanessa account and by the time he went to Vanessa's place Vanessa has disappeared with all his money, he was calling her and causing her to returned back his money, according to him he only transfered it to her because I called police for him, that was why he transfered all his money just for her to keep it until he was out of the mess, his account is empty he trusted her because they had plans and he love her that was why he trustee her enough to entrust all the Cash to her, the money he returned to me was borrowed with the hope he will get his money back and return the borrowed money to the owner, how will he be able to do that now that she has disappeared and refuse to say where she was... I watched as Denis pleaded, and Even threatens to kill her if she doesn't return his money, he was seriously threatening her and said so many thing but Vanessa did not show, he said to her the only thing in his name was the House and his car, he kept on begging Vanessa Who later blocked him and he couldn't reach her again on phone, he was pacing like a wounded Lion, helpless

he couldn't believe Vanessa could do such to him after all their plans,

Denis became so angry that period, I watched him hit the wall severally, out of frustration he even threw something at the downstairs big screened television and it shattered to the ground, I was watching with Binta who said that I should remain calm, his evil deed is catching up with him, he planned with Vanessa to duped me, and now the table has turned against him as Vanessa disappeared with all the money he transfered to her to keep, He thought he was smart and was planning with his partner in crime, not knowing his partner was having her own personal plans,

Denis stayed off my way so that I will not see how broken he was, I called my lawyer for the divorce paper, this was the perfect time to double strike him, a good time to useless his life, i will make sure even his car is collected from, I bought him the car and put his name on the house, I will tell My lawyer to make sure his name is out of my property, as I called my lawyer he said he was working on it, I should give him time,

Denis was so evil, how did My father cope with him, when he was his P.A, now I begin to understand why binta hated him, Binta saw through him, I was blinded in the love i had for him, I have never loved any Man the way I loved Denis, he use to be very loving, when my father died of over dose he was always there for me, I fell for him not knowing he was after all my father laboured for, he took advantage of me and he never truly loved me but loved only the things my father Left behind for me,

My CCTV revealed a whole lot of frightening things about Denis, I wouldn't have known or believed them if somebody had said that about Denis, seeing was believing, it was until I saw, heard and was played, when he lied to get money from me that I became scared, Denis was capable of anything.

Kuria stayed for two months instead of one before coming back, when Binta told me he was back, she went to his shop and one of his staffs said he came back yesterday, she visited his house and met a lady who greeted her and asked who she was, after introducing herself the girl said kuria was not around at the moment,

After hearing Binta say that my heart began to beat faster, the Lady in Kuria's house was probably his girlfriend or fiance that was why he stayed extra month, and didn't call as he returned, tears gathered in my eyes because I knew I have lost Kuria to another woman, may be this is my punishment for deeply loving the wrong person, I tried to hold back the tears but it flows more as i looked at my baby, I started Wondering why he didn't let me know that he was back,

I wanted to move on with my live but I kept on thinking about Kuria, I had his daughter, my Godsgift to me in my arms, looking at Luella was enough hope to move on,

One day Binta said we should just drive down to his place and find out if the Lady was his girlfriend before concluding,

I hesitated, I told her I can't face him knowing another woman is with him, she encouraged me to get dress let's go, I sluggishly did and we drove down, as we tapped on the door the Girl that Binta mentioned showed up at the door, smiling at us, she was a very young girl, maybe early twenties, i wanted to turn back, and drive back to My House with my baby on seeing the beautiful tall black young Girl, but Binta held me,

Binta asked of Kuria she smiled broadly and said he was inside, I stood at the door while Binta made a move to enter, Binta held me as went inside, she asked us to sit while she gets him, Binta sat and crossed her leg but I stood where I was,

Within second Kuria showed up the Lady was behind him, on seeing me, he rushed to me and drew and my baby into an embraced, which lasted for so long, he kissed my two cheeks out of Joy, I looked at the girl's face to see if she felt bad about Kuria hugging me but she was smiling,

Kuria carried Luella from me, laughing and apologizing that he was back since four days ago and planed to give me a surprise visit once he was done with his shop accounting Work, which kept him occupied, he also hugged Binta who was smiling, he said he has to stayed extra month because his mother was sick, but was feeling better before he came back,

I wasn't still comfortable having his girlfriend watch us and smile, he suddenly turned to me and asked the beautiful tall girl to come close, he introduced her as Mera, the girl he told me off, who was in a girls boarding school, I remembered Mera but I never met her, Mera was just 16years, but was so tall and beautiful with her shining black colour, Kuria picked Mera and Jude from the Street many years back and has being the father they never had,

Binta looked me after the introduction and started laughing I joined in because I felt so relived, Kuria didn't understand the laughter but kept on smiling, Binta asked Kuria what he was feeding Mera who was so Big for her age, Kuria laughed,

Mera came and took Luella from Kuria, Kuria took Luella from her and send her to get us drinks, and she replied Kuria with "yes uncle" just as Jude, Jude also came down and greeted us before going to assist Mera, Kuria sat beside me still carrying Luella as he gist us how his journey went, he told me he missed me so much and kissed my forehead, he asked of my husband, And i ignored the question, I told him I misses him too, he was so happy as held me and Luella as if we belonged to him,

I felt so happy but I need to find a perfect time to tell him that the baby girl in his arm was his own flesh and blood.

JODA, Episode 18.

My lawyer brought the divorce paper, and Denis on seeing I wasn't joking About divorcing him flared up, he became violent and started destroying things in the house, Denis asked my lawyer to leave,

I remain calm as he went about with his rage, Binta who was outside rushed in on hearing the whole noise, Denis walked Binta out, Binta refused to step out, he was trying to engage Binta into a fight, Binta was a strong willed person, she was also Strong physically, having gone through karate back in school, where she learnt defense moves, back then I use to Joke with her that her husband or boyfriend is in big trouble if she ever gets angry and she will laugh and say she only learnt how to defend herself from bad people out there and will never engage in a fight with her spouse,

As I watch her argue and held Denis from destroying things in the house I started wishing I have her kinds of strength and courage,

Luella woke and started crying, the noise woke her up, I rushed to My room and carried My Baby, I nursed her back to sleep.

The noise was becoming too much, I came out and saw Binta still holding Denis as he struggle, he kicked Binta hard on her stomach, she fell to the ground in pain, Denis Left and said before he returns back binta should make sure that she's gone,

I rushed to her she said she was fine but I can see she was in serious pain, I asked her to leave before Denis hurts her more, she said she wasn't leaving me and him alone I urged her, because i thought Denis won't be able to hurt me physically he can only destroy things and use words to spite me,

she stood up and said she will leave but she will be back in 30minute, Binta whispered something to my ear, she asked me to get my phone and put it on record, so that I can personally record every word Denis said to me, because he may tries to threatens me just as he did with Vanessa after she vanished with his money,

After Binta Left, i put my phone on recording and hide it within, when Denis came back he was a bit calm, he looked around at the things he has destroyed and sighed, he sat hard on the chair before looking at me

"How could you Joda, how could you do this to me, your husband and the father of your child, Luella my daughter Will never forgive you for doing this to her father, I Will make sure of that, and I will never sign that divorce paper, I will never.... you can go to hell with your lawyer, your stupid friend Binta, she was Lucky to leave I would have disfigured that her face that no Man will be able to marry her again, she was trying to show me she got the strength of a man, Not knowing she will always be woman, " weaker vessels " daughters of Jezebel, your friend Vanessa is the first daughter of the devil himself, women can never be trusted, very strange deceiving creatures, Joda you where naive and foolishly in love with me, you do My every bidding until Binta started influencing you, you allowed her because you can never make your own decision without being told what to do, you are that stupid, and you think you succeeded by giving me a divorce paper to sign, how foolish can you be, thinking I will sign the papers, since you plan to discard me after your friend Vanessa has done the worst by striping me naked and taking every dim I suffered for I will Tell you what that will break you into pieces, your Jezebel friend Vanessa was My whore, I used her Even in our matrimonial bed, I used her through out the night while you slept like a log of wood, then I used you in the morning for early morning tea, hahaha...Vanessa was so sweet, we even did it right in the the same bed with you after you passed out, Vanessa use to stuff her pants in to your mouth as you snore and I Will watch and laugh, I still own this house, and yes I collected 10million from you because you are too slow in putting my names in the other properties, you did not make me a signatory to the company's account or your father's, anytime I ask or remind you of it you will tell me to calm down because "your money is my money" how is that even possible when you are still in charge of everything, you became very stingy and wicked, all thanks to your stupid friend Binta, who you allowed to Wash your brain with her lies, I hate you Joda for making me to go through so much pain, my only Joy now is my daughter and you can never stop me from being in her life,

I listened to him talk and talk, he even tore the divorce paper into pieces, I didn't want to say much because I was recording, but when he said he hated me and talk about Vanessa, and then my daughter Luella as his hope in getting to me in the future I spoke

"Denis, you are a loser because all your plans has failed you, you said you hate me, hahahaha....that makes two of us, I hate you more my darling ex husband, now let me blow you away, I knew about your constant cheating with Vanessa that even made you to insist she Best me, I knew it even resulted to you drugging me so that you can feel safe during the night, and do your dirty deed right in my presence, yes all thanks to my Binta, is good to have a smart and reliable Friend not the one that Will betray me as Vanessa betrayed you and milk you dry, I know you Will be wondering how I got to know lots of things, well my wonderful Friend Binta is a prophetess, even if I'm naive and stupid my friend is wise and blunt, please get ready for another shocker, hahaha....i love this our confession, the only thing i learnt from You is how to cheat, yes my stupid and naïve self was feed up with your constant cheating, you never wondered how I managed to remain calm after accusing you of cheating with Vanessa, because you aren't my problem any more I was busy loving the right person which resulted to Luella, sorry to burst your bubbles, Luella is not your daughter, because you are a cursed being, I guess you are even impotent, all through the times I have being with you, even small pregnancy did not enter... Hahaha, I guess you don't Even use protection on Vanessa yet she never get pregnant, I so much thank God that very soon nothing will connect us both,

Denis was looking at me like he was in shock after hearing that Luella wasn't Even his daughter, he suddenly pounced on me and started hitting me, I fell to the ground, he asked me to repeat what I said about having affair and getting pregnant, I was in pain but I was glad that I hit him on the right spot i gladly repeated it, this time I added More spices so that it can be juicy, he kicked me and said it was a lie that I can't cheat on him, I don't have that nerve, I told him to Wait until Luella is a year old, I will do a DNA test to prove it to him, on hearing this Again he slapped me I managed to get up and hit him with the flower vase that was close to me, he staggered back as blood drip from his Head, he came Again at me and I try to struggled to get up and run into the room where I will be able to lock the door and call the police, but I couldn't get free, Denis was the devil him self as he hit me while shouting and calling me a harlot, and all kinds of name and then he said the last word that I almost fainted, Denis opened his mouth to my shock and said

"I will be so glad to kill you..so glad to kill you and your bastard child and end your generation, I started it with your stingy father...I killed him, yes...i did it.. Hahaha... Joda.you should really be scared of me because I'm capable of anything, oh Joda, no one crosses me and gets away with it...I Will kill you Joda like I did to your father... Your stingy father was nice in the beginning but changed later with the excuse that money wasn't forthcoming, I knew he has the money but suddenly became stingy and started focusing More on less important people, I was his P.A, i deserved more than he was offering me, well when I couldn't Bear it any more I started adding some killer drugs to his coffee and drinks, gradually it was eating his lungs and intestine, I did that without care, unsuspicious, because he trusted me, I did it gradually watching him wrath in pain until he died, I knew you Are next in Line...I needed to get to your heart...I saw your weak point and did all I could until you couldn't do without me, I'm a winner my darling wife, you and your father are fools, you can't take my word to anywhere because nobody Will believe you, no evidence, naïve spoit brat like you... I will..

He was still talking when the door was kicked open Binta and Kuria came in, on seeing Kuria he attacked him, saying he was the one all this while that i was having affair with, which resulted to My pregnancy, Denis caused and throw punches at

Kuria, Kuria dodged his blows and slapped and kicked him and he fell to the ground, Binta was holding me I needed to unhear that Denis really killed my father, Binta was telling me that the Police where on the way, Kuria came to me but I kicked everyone screaming, I was crying my head was heavy my heart was shattered, I wanted to revenge my dad's death, I was going crazy as I scattered my Hair and tore my cloth... Oh the pain in my heart was too much to Bear...my body was soaked with tears and sweat, I felt pain from Denis beating but it can't be compared to the heaviness in my heart...my father was killed by Denis, I actually fell in love with my father's killer and married him...just that realization alone was enough to kill me...

JODA, Episode 19.

Denis was charged to court, there was enough evidence to nail him, the phone recording help a great deal, and also the house CCTV, he couldn't alter a word because he knew everything was working against him, Even his lawyer was left speechless, he signed all the necessary papers, including the divorce paper, i collected everything I put in his name include the House and his car, he was stripe and tortured, at the end Denis was sentence to 56years in prison with hard labour,
The Police where in search of Vanessa and she was later found, because she was an accomplice and she and Denis teamed up to drug me and also rob

me off 10million, which he later return 5million, Vanessa was sentence to 4years in prison without bail.

After they were put behind bars I wasn't still myself, I cried everyday and I refuse to see any Man, even Kuria, Binta was the only person I allowed close, I was constantly visiting my father's grave to beg for his forgiveness, I had a choice to choose wisely but I chooses wrongly, I began to see meaning in the dream I once had, that father suddenly appeared to stop the wedding between me and Denis, I saw all the warning sign, I should have being able to know something was not just right, I should have known but how blinded in love I was, oblivious to things around me, I hated myself, I don't know how to forgive myself, I live in guilt and pain,

Binta was trying to console me but it did no good, I told Kuria to stay away, I don't know how to love or trust another man, if Denis could turn out to be the devil himself then I should be careful with men,

I knew Kuria was coming everyday but stays down to talk with Binta and play with his daughter, Luella.

The sadness was too much, the fear, the pains and regrets was what I fed on for three months, I started mourning Fathers death all over, I wore mostly black dresses, guilt was eating at me, anytime I thought of Denis, killing my dad gradually without him even knowing, until he finally died of overdose, and I gladly fell in love and married a murderer, it was just too painful, I gradually started losing weight, I couldn't take proper Care of Luella, Binta took over the motherhood thing from me, sometime she carries Luella down to meet Kuria who I banned from seeing me, they stayed there for hours, I like it More when there's nobody to tell me to stop crying, i like to stare at an empty space and imagine how I messed up my own life, how it would have being if father was still alive, or Even mother, how easy it would have being if I wasn't the only child, how pleasant if I have a family member close by, I felt so lonely and weak, father Left so much behind for me, I can't even spend anything without guilt, it was his sweat I was lavishing on Denis, how could I do such a foolish thing? what could I have done without Binta who was practically my only companion, my only friend who turned out to be mean everything, Binta was my only family. I grew weaker everyday, I became flesh and bone, I started hating my house because it reminds me of Denis

"Joda, do you want to kill yourself, is this how you want to end up, your father will not forgive you if you cut off his lineage, you made a mistake, let's thank God for his correction rod, God saved you from Denis because you are very important to him, show some gratitude to him for revealing this at his own time, stop beating yourself, your baby needs you, I need my Joda, and please stop punishing Kuria for Denis mistake, Kuria loves you and it hurt him every time you pushes him off and wouldn't see him, Kuria is patient and he never stops praying for you, please see Kuria, he is going crazy Joda... Please.. I'm begging you snap out of this, please allow him in...please..

" Binta... Denis killed my father, I married the man that murdered My father, I don't know how to live with myself... I...I...is just too painful Binta...

" I understand how painful it could be, stop eating yourself up, stop hurting yourself, please...time will heal all wound, you have to learn to forgive yourself, i know your father will love to see you bounce back, be a strong woman, let this build you up and not weakens you, you are saved just in time Joda, please stop punishing Kuria with the sins of Denis, Kuria truly loves you...I need my friend back, Luella wants her mummy back, God works perfectly well, he didn't allow any offspring to come from Denis, he will spend almost all his life in a cell, he will die lonely and a sad Man, he will have regrets at the end but it will be too late because no time to correct his past mistake, he had opportunity to be better but he decided to sell his soul to the devil, God is still our judge... He will never allow the wicked to go unpunished, God fight for the weak and innocent, he fought for you and defended you from Denis, Denis is under the law and nothing could save him, except if God decides to have mercy on him, but I know the wicked will never go Scot free, even the law can't save them if God opens their Case.. Get up and take away this black dress... is time to start another phrase...
Binta talks and I paid attention because God has used her to save me severally, she was smart and filled with wisdom, I got up but I was too weak to stand, i fell back to the bed, Binta shouted Kuria Who was carrying Luella downstairs to come he was up within a second, he handed Luella to Binta on seeing me, Binta told him to take to the hospital, he lifted me up, I was like a feather in his arm and rushed me to his car, Binta followed suit carrying Luella, I was rushed to the hospital where I was

admitted, Kuria Sat beside me and held my hand while the doctor administer drugs and drips..
Within a month I was fine and Free to go home, I started working on recovering, Kuria and Binta did all they could to put Smile on my face, it felt so good having this two wonderful friends around, I cherished their company.
For the first time in 7months I laughed so hard from Kuria's Joke, I started loving him all over again, and when we finally shared a deep kiss, it felt so good, he asked me why i never told him about Luella, he was sad that I kept such thing away from him, he deserved to know that i was carrying his child, I quickly apologized and explain my reasons, Which he understood. I fell in love all over again with him. And thanked him for his loving patient.
Binta has a good news, she and James will be wedding in three months time, I was happy for her and told her not to bother about the expenses I will foot it all, she rejected my offer and said she and James have done a lot of savings towards the wedding which wasn't a Big wedding, James will love to spend from his savings to make her proud, I understand Binta so I decide not to push further,
After a month of Binta's Good news, Kuria asked me to marry him, I felt safe and loved but I couldn't say yes immediately, I needed to make sure I was ready for another marriage, I didn't want to hurt kuria because of my past, I wanted to be sure that I was healed from safe hurt, so I asked him to give me time, which he did, kuria was always patient with me and never rushes me up, and just within two weeks I know there was no better Man for me than Kuria,

Our wedding was on same month with Binta and James, since my wedding was a week before Binta, I begged her with a brown new car to Best me, she was so happy and was willing to hand me over to the Man that is meant for me, it wasn't a big wedding like my previous but it was exactly what I wanted, our little daughter Luella was our ring bearer

After we were pronounced as husband and wife, I suddenly burst out crying because it took me lost, pain and a difficult journey to finally arrive at the right place, I felt God's kind of love where I was, i imagined my father smiling down at me and saying "Joda, you finally did the Right thing... I'm so proud of you my daughter"...

THE FINAL EPISODE OF JODA.

9years has already gone by since I got married to Kuria, Kuria has being an Angel, he isn't perfect, some days we have misunderstanding, when we can't agree on one thing, but I assure it never passes that day, I have never gone to bed sad because Kuria makes sure I'm always happy,

I always makes sure he does not go to bed sad, I love him too much to see him sad or worried,

We act More like friends, joking and laughing at ourselves, I'm glad I married my Friend, if i have to choose again, I will choose Kuria all over.

We are blessed with 3kids, Luella and her two brothers are one of my biggest blessing

After Binta's wedding I gave her a surprised gift, the big house I once shared with Denis, was their weddings gift,
Kuria's decoration on it grows finer everyday, but I feel so empty being in that House because it reminds me of my past, and because I didn't want to sale the house I gave it to Binta and her husband, James.
i have being looking for a perfect Gift for Binta to show her how grateful and honored I was to have some body like her as a friend, friends like hers are rare to find, having her in my life has being a blessing, I came to a conclusion with Kuria and gave her the house, putting her name on it as the sole owner, she cried a bucketful of tears after I surprised her And her husband James, James thought it was a joke until my lawyer arrive with the papers and they signed as owners, it was the least I could do for her after she has being the only person I called a friend Who turn out to be more than a sister, God brought another friend, Kuria in to my life, who ended up being my husband and the father of my kids.
I live with Kuria in his beautiful warm House, it wasn't so big like my previous house but it was a home, Binta had two kids within 9years,
after having her first child, a boy, she tried getting pregnant but it was difficult, there was a delay with her second children, she prayed to have just one again to make it two, I also joined her in praying, she prayed for a girl, and her girl came after seven years of birthing her first child, her Joy was full as she closes the chapter of birth,

We gather every weekend to eat one of Kuria delicacy, which I have learnt almost all but mine never tastes like Kuria, he had a magic hand that beautifies and add taste to everything he touches,
Mera got engaged and Kuria acted like her father, he walked her down and handed her over to her husband, everybody got emotional, it was a beautiful sight to behold, I loved Mera like my sister, we showered her with a lot of gifts, she cried and hugged Kuria, thanking him for being a parent she never had, I was happy when I watch Kuria walk her down the aisle, I know someday he will also walk Luella down, handing her over to a good man like him, until then I will prepare my daughter to be every man's dream, to be kind and loving.
Our kids are growing everyday in strength and wisdom, I joined hand with him in saving the street kids, we did the Best we can because we know that is impossible to save the world, we built an orphanage home where most of them are kept and cared for by abled hands we employed,
it was a Big project indeed but I was glad to be making good use of the resources that I have, Kuria had a Big heart and he loved children, being his wife, the mother of his children and working with him was a great privilege I wouldn't trade for anything, he was an Angel in human form.
We have visited his mother three times and she has flew down twice to see us, she has has being a blessing, she became the mother I never had, she was so loving like her son, oh before I forget she was beautiful inside out just like her son too.
Vanessa was out of prison after 4years, she came begging for my forgiveness, she was remorseful

and regretted her past life and I totally forgave her, and gave her a job in my father's company for her to be able to start her life all over, which won't be easy after being behind bars for almost five years, but I know she will be fine,

I visited my father's grave with Kuria and the kids last month and I felt the need to go visit Denis and to let him know that I have forgiven him, I knew my father was a loving and very accommodating man, he wouldn't want me to hold unforgiveness in my heart, it was time to be totally free, time to face the dreaded moment I have always being scared of, Kuria asked me if I was sure of doing it, after he drove me down, I assured him again for the 4th time that day that I can do it, he waited for me at the parking slot, since it was my battle I will face it alone,

I waited at the visitors hall until the wardens brought him out in chains, he didn't know who had come to seen him, because he hardly gets visitors, his hair was turning White, his bears was growing all over his face, I guest he hasn't shaved for a very Long time, he was looking malnourished, he looked too old more than his age, he has already spent 10 years in prison, remaining 46years, I sat there looking at him and allowing forgiveness and kindness to sulk me in, I kept the door of bitterness shot, I knew I was doing the right thing, It wasn't Binta or kuria that told me to do this, I decided on my own, I made this decision, i will stick to it no matter how it hurts,

Denis scanned with his eyes at the visitors seated who has come to see their love ones, I sat watching him look from face to face until his eyes settled on me, he blinks twice,wanting to make sure that I was the one, I was just seating and watching him, I wasn't smiling, and I wasn't wearing an angry look either, I was just neutral, he paused as he got closer and breathed deeply, before coming to sit opposite me,

no need to ask him how he was doing because I know how terrible a prison can be and it was obviously written on him, we kept quiet for sometime, his head was Bent and he later said

"Joda....You are the last person I expected to see here, I have being praying, i repented and turned a new leaf years back, I have being praying for so many years now for God to grant me another chance to plead for your forgiveness Joda, I never gave up asking and praying and I will totally understand God if he choose to ignore me, because I know I don't deserve anything good, but on seeing you I knew God finally hard me, I don't Care how many years I survive here before dying but I Will die peacefully knowing that I was able to see you and begged to be forgiven..... sorry is used frequently that we forget the importance of it, i misused the word" sorry " I was evil and self centered, I know, I carried the weight of it right in my heart every day, I don't deserve to be forgiven, I don't deserve any thing at all from you, not even your presence here, I was greedy and became the devil Joda, I know my terrible deeds before I was Even sentenced, I know I deserve death, I suppose to be sentence to death but God gave me a chance to find my footing and opportunity to see you again after so many years, I lost count of years in here, you look good and happy too, I'm glad, God really got you Joda....forgive me please, give me this only thing I seek which is your forgiveness so that when I die I Will die knowing I finally made Peace with you, my soul and conscience will find Mercy... Please Joda....

I watched him, looking deeply at my father's killer, who tricked me into marrying him so that he can have all that my father laboured for during his lifetime, but Denis has changed, he wasn't the same person any more, as tears drop from his eyes, years has changed him, he was really sorry, my father used to love him like the son he never had, until he begin to want More than my father could offer, the things he wanted and killed to get are the same thing he will leave behind when he dies, so why fight so much for what you can not take along with you to the grave, tears gathered in my eyes but i blinked it back, I kept on blinking back tears,

I held his hand urging him to look up at me, which he did, I smile and reassure him that I have already forgiven him before coming down to see him, all I wanted to do was to say it to his face,

He smiled and breathed deeply again, before saying thank you, we talk a little while before the Police guards came and took him away,

I stood, watching him go, he turned back again and muttered a silent"thank you " I smile and nodded before they locked the iron door, i finally heaped a sigh of relief before walking out,

I felt this inner fulfillment and Joy, as I came out of the prison Yard I sprayed out my hands wide and look in to the sky and said thank you to the invisible being up there, who has always seeing me through

Sometimes forgiveness does More good to the Victim, than with the offender, I felt so good, I forgave myself before being able to forgive others, it was a long process for me, gradually I did it.
I was feeling proud and I know Father Will be More proud,
As I entered the car, Kuria who has being waiting for me, asked me how it went, I smiled and hugged him, he held me like he has done for years, I allowed all the tears I held back to flow,
Everyone deserves a companion like Kuria and a true friend like Binta, with this two kind of people who will love and guide you through life, you Will always have reasons to smile.

The end.